The Sleep of the Great Hypnotist

By Peter Redgrove

The Collector and Other Poems
  Routledge & Kegan Paul

The Nature of Cold Weather and Other Poems
  Routledge & Kegan Paul

At The White Monument and Other Poems
  Routledge & Kegan Paul

The Force and Other Poems
  Routledge and Kegan Paul

Work in Progress (Poems 1969)

The Hermaphrodite Album (with Penelope Shuttle)

Dr Faust's Sea-Spiral Spirit and Other Poems
  Routledge & Kegan Paul

In the Country of the Skin
  Routledge & Kegan Paul

The Terrors of Dr Treviles: A Romance
(with Penelope Shuttle)
  Routledge & Kegan Paul

Sons of My Skin: Redgrove's Selected Poems 1954-74
  Routledge & Kegan Paul

The Glass Cottage: A Nautical Romance
(with Penelope Shuttle)
  Routledge & Kegan Paul

From Every Chink of the Ark and Other New Poems
  Routledge & Kegan Paul

The Wise Wound (with Penelope Shuttle)

The God of Glass: A Morality
  Routledge & Kegan Paul

The Weddings at Nether Powers and Other New Poems
  Routledge & Kegan Paul

The Sleep of the Great Hypnotist

The Life and Death and Life After Death
of a Modern Magician

Peter Redgrove

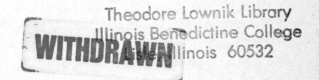

Routledge & Kegan Paul
London and Henley

First published in 1979
by Routledge & Kegan Paul Ltd.
39 Store Street, London WC1E 7DD and
Broadway House, Newtown Road,
Henley-on-Thames, Oxon RG9 1EN
Set in IBM Baskerville 11 on 12pt by Columns
and printed in Great Britain by
Lowe and Brydone Ltd.

All the incidents and characters in this book are the
invention of the author. Any similarity to any person
living or dead is completely unintentional.

British Library Cataloguing in Publication Data

Redgrove, Peter
The sleep of the great hypnotist.
I. Title
823'.9'1F   PR6035.E267S/
ISBN 0 7100 0310 2

Acknowledgments

Grateful acknowledgments are due to the Plymouth Theatre Company's lunchtime play-commission of *The Hypnotist*, in which the theme of Blind Man and Hypnotist, which occurs in Part One of this novel, was varied for stage performance.

The novel originated in the same author's poem 'The Sleep of the Great Hypnotist', printed in his *From Every Chink of the Art and Other Poems* (Routledge & Kegan Paul, 1977).

Contents

PART ONE

The Blind Seer

'Shit!' said the Great Hypnotist to the Medical Congress as the wasp stung the hand that was lifted in a potent pass. Sir Alexander Pocket in the front row stared at him with sleeping eyes. A warm smell of distinguished human manure filled the room.

Now it is in all the books, mentioned slyly, how, in the middle of his demonstration to a recalcitrant body of medical men and women, in which he had succeeded in lulling his opposition into a state of blissful trance, George Frederick Pfoundes, that Great Hypnotist, due to the intervention of a virile and angry wasp, gave out a most embarrassing expletive. There were thirty distinguished medicos in the room. They shat, on command. They sat there, with blissful smiles, like babies in warm and companionable nappies. The stable smells filled the air. Pfoundes paused. How should he phrase his next command? 'Now you are in a lift that is descending. You look up at the little panels above the door that light up as you descend through the floors, gliding down silently, fast and easily. They light up brightly, with dark letters on the light squares. 21 . . . 20 . . . 19 . . . You are going down, down, down, and as you go down you are more and more deeply relaxed. You hear my voice, and my voice only, and the hum and swish of the oiled machinery as you descend into deeper and deeper relaxation. 18 . . . 17 . . . 16 . . . Soon you will

3

reach the ground floor and the doors will open for you and you will walk slowly out of this room, slowly and carefully, and you will enter the hotel lobby, and without speaking you will enter another lift and you will go to your hotel room where you will take a bath. 4 ... 3 ... 2 ... 1 ... Ground floor.'

Slowly, as one person, the delegates got up, walking carefully, and left the conference room by the large doors at the back. As the room emptied in silence, Pfoundes stood on the platform, the Pfoundes Oscilloscope, the Hypnosis machine that he had invented, humming and sparkling with its coloured pictures on the table at his side. 'Oh,' he thought to himself, 'I forgot to tell them to forget . . .' and 'Oh! what a good thing I didn't say "Bugger!" when the wasp stung my hand!'

* * *

The consulting-room has unusual decorations. There is a big office desk by an open window, an upright chair behind it, an easy chair in the space before the desk, and facing the easy chair another upright one, with curved legs. There is a small magazine table, and a hatstand. There is a sideboard on which the Pfoundes Oscilloscope sits, like a television set with three screens. Its quadrophonic speakers are stapled to the walls.

It is these walls that are the oddity. Instead of the normal, repeated wallpaper patterns — the blue and ribbon-tied bouquets of flowers usual to a Harley Street consulting-room, or the rather more severe Augustan white and gold that goes with little gilt chairs — there is a great swirl of colours on these walls.

4

A purple swathe begins in one corner of the ceiling and travels twisting and rising into a yellow torrent of colour that pours across the ceiling plaster. From a crimson circle, blood-colours jet across to the tall windows, and swerve round underneath the carpet. Green coils around the purple swathe, and gold nets flash over the red. Caught within the yellow stream are shapes like birds and blind fishes. All the shapes circumscribe but do not precisely define an implied centre. The Great Hypnotist sits at his impersonal desk by the window, and his head with its flashing eyes and great chin supplies the exact focus that the diagram omits. The room aches in colour for his presence. When he is not there, it is gaudy. As he sits in it, it is hypnotic. Pfoundes presses a bell-push on his desk. After a short pause, there are tapping noises with an occasional clatter as of a stick striking panelling at the turn of a corridor. The tapping moves closer. There is a loud rapping at the door.

'Come in!'

The handle turns slowly and the door swings open. There is a man with dark glasses and a white stick on the threshold.

'May I come in?'

'Come in!'

The blind man does not move from the threshold.

'Is this the Hypnotist?'

'Yes, this is he. I am over here.'

The blind man pauses still. But evidently the hypnotist is not going to get up and help him into the room.

'Would you please make another remark?'

'I will sing if you like,' says Pfoundes, 'or swear, or tell you a bedtime story.'

5

The blind man sways slightly to the savagery in Pfoundes' voice, but takes his decision, and with sliding footsteps moves forward. His white antenna or wand is made of steel, and is telescopic, making no sound as it sweeps out a path to and fro for him across the deep red carpet. There is a click as it catches the magazine table, and he changes course slightly, pausing and turning his nose about, the nostrils tilted up like deep black tunnels at the end of which there may be eyes. He smiles.

'I like an open window when the sun is shining.'

'Please sit down,' says Pfoundes, watching him carefully.

'I must get my bearings.'

'There is an easy chair!' Pfoundes speaks loudly. The blind man looks directly at him with his nostrils, then swiftly turns his head, listening.

'I am blind, you know.'

'I like to see how a man handles himself.'

Again Pfoundes' voice is loud, as if his patient were deaf, not blind. And the blind man now shuffles over the carpet directly towards the easy chair, his thin metal stick radaring the way. He reaches the chair, bends over it, feels it out with his fingers, takes a grip on the arms and lowers himself into the seat. Pfoundes looks at him with interest.

'Please take your hat off.'

The blind man does so; his hair is yellow, but dark with sweat. He takes out a handkerchief and wipes his face and neck, and pats it over the crown of his head. Pfoundes watches him. Dr Pfoundes has a large squarish head, his hair is black and slicked down as befits a Harley Street man. He wears a black coat and striped trousers, his collar is stiff and white, but his tie repeats the amazing swirling pattern on

6

the consulting-room wall, of yellow, crimson, purple and gold.

'I have heard that you can help blind people.'

'What have you heard?'

'That by a course of hypnotic treatment you can so improve their sensitivity to sightless clues in the environment that they seem almost to see. You *saw* how difficult it was for me to find this chair I am sitting in. The room was strange to me.'

'I saw.'

'But I found it.'

'Tell me how you found it.'

'I have been blind for twenty years. I have trained myself to feel, to listen and to smell. That window sends forth a stream of cool air that is to me like a lamp shedding rays of light. But these rays bend and curl round objects, and convey the smells of things as they travel, just as light is stained with colours when it passes through church glass. That beam of air from the window casts wind-shadows of all the obstacles in this room, making patterns of odour, making patterns of cold and warmth I can feel on my skin.'

Pfoundes opens a box on his desk and takes out a cigar. He rustles the cigar into his ear by rolling it between finger and thumb.

'Oh yes,' says the blind man cheerfully, 'do light up your cigar. It will not hinder me, as perhaps you think it will. It too will curl its strong brown odour made of rain forests and mahogany board-rooms round all the objects in this room. Why do you not smoke it standing up, on this side of the desk, as you usually do? Here —' he points to a place where the yellow wall-torrent thins into a perspective of green cones — 'the wallpaper still carries the smell-print of

7

your smoking.'

Pfoundes looks hard at the blind man in his rain-coat lounging in the easy chair, and puts the cigar back in its box.

'I know where you are sitting because you use shaving lotion. It is Brut shaving lotion. The passage of air past your cheeks draws out a long-body or echo of your face which is smeared across the room. You have been sitting still at that desk for some while because the flags and trailers of smell in the room from your shaved face are nearly faded away. They are like torn cobwebs. The mask of perfume whose outer fringes enter my nostrils as though your whole face were kissing me, hangs over your desk, only a little bloated and smeared by your fairly deliberate considering movements as you study your papers and speak; and I know it is a desk because your voice booms in its wooden chambers in a manner which suggests to me a fairly cheap job in elm with a whitebeam veneer, and that you keep a tape-recorder in the bottom right-hand drawer because I can hear its motor, and paperclips in the top left-hand one because the lower register of your voice rubs them with tiny screeches across each other, minutely vibrated.'

'Are you some sort of poet?'

'Could I afford your fee if I were?'

'Max Carrados, the blind detective?'

'He died many years ago. Dr Pfoundes, I have been told that you are a gruff and blunt man, but also that you are a great doctor. When you spoke so loudly as if to frighten me, that simply left a pattern of echoes like a radar-map in the air. I heard the faint hum of springs in the seat of the easy-chair.'

'Try this then!' Pfoundes opens the drawer of his

desk which contains the tape-recorder, takes out a microphone, and points it like a magic wand at one of the big loudspeakers that are stapled to the wall of the consulting-room. There is a fearful howl that gains in strength until the blind man is crouched shivering in his chair with hands held over his ears. Tears are streaming from beneath his dark glasses. Pfoundes pulls the microphone away from its direction, and the howl dies away. He crosses from behind his desk and sits in the upright chair opposite the blind man, whose head is in his hands, and whose shoulders are shaking. Pfoundes reaches forwards under the trembling hands and eases the dark glasses off the man's face. He tilts the chin and looks at the eyes as the hands fall away. The lids are closed over them, and he cannot tell whether there is any eyeball in the socket, for though they are deeply sunken there is some fullness to them. They are circled with bruises, deep blue-black in colour, as though the face were deeply fatigued or recently dead. Tears well from between the tightly-closed lids. Pfoundes takes the weeping face in his hands and with finger and thumb tries to open the eyelids, but cannot. The blind man holds them so strongly shut (though the tears penetrate them) that without actually poking his finger in on the assumption that there are no eyeballs to be damaged Pfoundes cannot complete his examination. The blind man twists his head, taking deep breaths now as he recovers from the howl. Before he can complain, Pfoundes speaks.

'You walk among shadows and echoes. I could make you see those perfumes, those shadows and those echoes. You are good, but not as good as you could be. I could put eyes not only in your fingers but over your whole skin. I could give your ears eyes and your nostrils too. I could make you see.'

'How could I see!'

'As in a dream.'

'I have beautiful dreams of when I could see.'

'You shall have these dreams awake. It will be because I've taught you to see the sounds directly as images, and to image the touches of warm and cold air on your skin. You shall see all your loved ones, now twenty years older, but loving still . . .'

'My sight . . .?'

'You shall see your loved ones in your mind's eye.'

'But I do already . . .'

'As they speak and as they smell and as they feel to your fingertips.'

'I shall see . . .'

'But not with your eyes.'

'What is this hypnotism? Is it magic?'

'No. Though all magic is hypnotism. You have already experienced hypnotism.'

'In my magic moments?'

'Precisely. You know those times when you are falling asleep, you are very heavy, very relaxed, you are stretched out in the bed and you are utterly comfortable, there is no need to move or fidget, it is utter peace, you are at one with yourself, sleep will come when it's ready, but this is neither sleeping nor waking, but between the two.'

'It is so beautiful when that happens.'

'Just so. And you know you are not dreaming because you can feel with your skin the warmth of the bed and the roughness of the sheets and the caress of your nightclothes; but just beyond, somewhere both inside and outside, the dreams are beginning to well up, and in your sense of the real bed, the real body, you are nevertheless hovering over the well

10

of dreams, like that pool which still trembles with its currents and swirlings even though there is no wind and the sky is blue and still.'

'I can see it now . . .'

'And that is my point.'

'You are hypnotising me.'

'I am hypnotising you by telling you what the experience of hypnotism is, how everyone experiences it, and how all we need is practice to enlarge that blissful experience between sleeping and waking in which we have the abilities of both sleeping and waking. Our scientists call these states hypnagogic or hypnopompic according to whether you experience them as you are going to sleep or just waking up, in that blissful relaxation when your dreams are echoes and the world on which you open your eyes is not yet spoilt, but what the Tantrists call the state of the Mother Clear Birth Light, because that is where everything is new-made . . .'

'How beautiful . . .'

'Yes, including eyes. Including sight.'

'I am beginning to see what you mean. In that twilight zone, if I hear a noise in the street, it will either wake me, or . . .'

'Or it will turn into a beautiful expanding cantata, the words said will echo exploring their meanings, *Mother, I'm home* shouts the adolescent at twelve-thirty at night, not only in order that his mother may know, but the whole street as well, but your Mother Clear Birth State echoes and re-forms the words in the great sea-conch of your attention *Mother, myther of me, I hum that I'm home in the Om where I am the Aum*: Listen!'

Pfoundes has in his hand a small flat plastic box which is studded with switches. It is a remote-control

11

device, for when he presses on it, the screens of the Pfoundes Oscilloscope on the sideboard begin to flicker into colour patterns that resemble the large swirling shapes with which Pfoundes has decorated his consulting-room and his necktie. A slight hum comes from the four speakers stapled to the room's walls.

'Listen! *Mother, I'm home!*' and he presses another switch.

A chord of music comes from the Oscilloscope speakers, as though the keys of a great organ had been pressed in a slow sequence. Behind the burdoun there is a high *vox humani* figure which gathers together under the bass notes which throb in unison *Moth, Moth, Moth, Her, Her, Her, I am, I am, Om, Om, I am,* and the large mythic voice like enormous lips moving slowly says the *I Am* as though a kindly God were speaking from the Burning Bush since a tiny piccolo stop now imitates the flaming and crackling of wood and the shrill desert wind that blows through the twigs, making the fire dance. Pfoundes twists a switch on the box and the music dies away.

'So you see that the state of hypnosis is a perfectly natural one, even though I may use a machine to amplify that state in you by a process of feedback, which is what happened when the microphone and the speaker howled at you. By pointing the microphone at the speaker I picked up the mains-hum and amplified it at the same time through the speaker and the amplified hum was picked up by the microphone which returned it to the speaker which returned it to the microphone raising it *ad infinitum* to the sound of a soul howling in agony containing all possible sounds in a white noise that for you was Hell itself.

I filled your sensitive blind ears with white noise and I have rinsed them and purged them and now I am telling you the truth that will be with you for the rest of your life, and will give you your sight again.'

'I am recovering from that noise . . .'

'Recovering from that noise you are in the state of Mother Clear Birth Hearing, having woken from the little nightmare I gave you. And what I have said for a sound heard in the street as you hover between sleeping and waking goes for a touch too, that will run all through your skin and your whole body, you will touch the breast of your blind girlfriend huddled in the blackness beside you and that shape will run along your arm and into your deepest being where the shape "a woman's breast" has lived almost since your earliest beginnings. And if you bury your nose in her perfumed hair, you are walking through the trunks of a scented forest.'

'But I have had these experiences as I make love to her, and I have been in that Mother Clear Birth Light after my intercourse with her, all passion spent . . .'

'Exactly. That is hypnotism. And the baby of eight months laughing at his rusk, chortling at the tempest-tossed forest of the crackling of a paper-bag, is in a state of hypnotism. Wouldn't it be better to say, though, that the person who is hypnotised is in the baby-state, interested in the Great Hypnotist in the Sky, the Greatest Hypnotist of All, Life itself whose fringes are all you can touch, like an old man dipping his toe in a blue Mediterranean tide, unless you are hypnotised in blissful relaxation. Plunge in, my dear friend, plunge in to life.'

The blind man's tight-pressed lids have begun to relax, and once Pfoundes glimpsed a flash of white between them, as though he were looking at a sighted man whose eyes had been rolled back into the forehead. The flow of tears has ceased, and Pfoundes takes his immaculate white handkerchief from his breast pocket and gently wipes his client's face. There is a smile on the blind face, and Pfoundes knows that now is the time to begin his hypnotic induction proper and to deepen the trance so that he can effectively treat his patient. He will use the Pfoundes Oscilloscope, though he cannot employ the visual feedback operation, which is so effective with sighted people. Nevertheless he will turn on the screens and the machine will as usual improvise sloweddown visual images fed to it by the tiny television cameras positioned round the room. A computer in the Oscilloscope rings the changes on the colour-harmonics and a telerecording device slows the images down and spreads them out, so that the visual process of falling asleep is reproduced on the screens, improvised on the basis of pictures taken from all round the person of the patient. This includes his own body movements. The fed-back impression of falling asleep produces the actual sensations as of falling asleep, which are again fed back: more important, the dreamlike improvisations produced by the machine rouse in the hypnotisee exactly those relaxed inventions which are characteristic of hypnagogic and hypnopompic states. Strange countries are seen in the swirling patterns, plants and beasts never before seen in the world, loved faces and unknown countenances grimacing and smiling. If the sound-channel of the Oscilloscope is turned on as well, the hypnotist's commands are enlarged and made sleepy, made musical, by the microphones that pick them up, as are the sounds of the room and the tiny movements of the hypnotist and sleeper. Strange

14

words are uttered by the machine, strange symphonies; and the trance grows deeper and deeper. In this state of complete receptivity anything that is said becomes a picture, anything seen becomes a sound, for in this trance, as in the state between sleeping and waking, all the senses are one sense, just as when you touch your closed eyelids with a finger you see a streak of light, you can see the touch of that finger. A blind man in that state of trance could see the face of his lady by the touch of her breath on his cheek.

Pfoundes will now introduce into his patient's trance strong and bizarre images of auto-erotic sensation, in order to arouse the skin. Pfoundes' shock-tactics are partly to please himself, but he uses them also because they are very effective. It is not so much that he is a cruel man. He is not basically and fundamentally cruel. It is that he is impatient. He is a man in whom life rushes at a great rate. He is a man who has released life-energies in himself by the practice of what the public finally calls hypnotism, but which they would call magic if they knew him better. The consequence of his experiments has been to take him in a rush to the peak of his profession, but he can find few people who, as it were, move at the same speed as his physical energies and his inner life. This makes him impatient and confident to the point of cruelty. It makes him seem elite also; yet he is not elitist. He knows that these energetic torrents are within everybody, waiting to be released by the techniques he has mastered.

* * *

The first person to hypnotise George Pfoundes was his Uncle Freddie. Frederick, his mother's only

15

brother, glittered. His hair was grey but bright as fuse-wire, his eyes black as buttons and turning everywhere. He had a glittering watch-chain across a waistcoat fastened with glittering buttons. His shoes sparkled in the fairylights, for Christmas was the only time of year that small George saw his uncle.

Frederick was a keen amateur conjurer whose forte was to surprise young children. He loved to hold them fascinated with card and ribbon tricks. He was never happier than when he looked round him at all the children open-mouthed at some audacity. Would the chosen card be found, miraculously dry, inside the cut lemon? How could more paper flowers emerge from that empty tin cylinder? The hush that greeted his tricks was to him, as ordinary time stopped, a religious moment.

And so it was for the children who watched him. What every child knew to be the true nature of the world was revealed to be an understanding also of the right kind of grown-up. There was a place below the world where rabbits burrowed, and sometimes they would have their thresholds in the golf-course or in the Home Park, and sometimes their front doors would be an old top hat or a painted Chinese box. Of course doves flew through ordinary matter as easily as they flew in the air; one needed to make them visible, that was all, or to give them entrances into our world, our time. Fire from matches could never destroy the best handkerchief lent by Aunt Edith, her treasured lace: it could if you were not a magician, but if you were, you knew how to burn things so that they could fly undamaged to the other side of the room and be found again inside a letter sealed with three great red seals. The most

16

precious things could be destroyed, and be found again. George Pfoundes at five years old knew many things that were magic in this way, but few grown-ups, in his opinion, paid proper attention to them, or dealt with them with the correct mixture of wonder and panache, or had the words that went fast enough and marvellously enough to help the magic along.

'I want you to watch very very carefully, ladies and gentlemen' (none of the ladies and gentlemen had passed their sixth year) 'while I load this old Chinese pistol that was given to me by the Mandarin Fu Manchu in his toadstool laboratory beneath the Hindu Kush.' Uncle Fred was manipulating an antique pistol that he had polished up so that its black barrel and brass mountings glittered like his shoes, like the little jewels of sweat on his high, sallow forehead. 'I load it, please notice, with pepper and salt, for this is a magic charge, and you know how fiery the pepper is, and how sharp your tears taste. Now, laying my loaded gun carefully on the table and keeping one eye on it at all times, I will unhinge my black box that I stole from the mad Arab Abdul Ahrazed under the stars of an Egyptian night while he lay in an opium trance in the middle of his harem of Amazon ladies, the least of whom could have broken the back of a tiger.' At this he picked up a wooden cube and placed it on a stand, tapped it with his conjurer's wand, dead black and tipped with ivory-white at both ends, and by opening all four sides showed that it was not only empty, but had that excellent air of non-existence that magical tools should have, being unfastenable in odd ways, more thoroughly empty than ordinary boxes, with more doors than any domestic utensil or toy, closing more secretly than common objects, and seemingly

17

bigger inside when they were closed than they were when open.

Small George could see everything that his uncle said. The pistol, with its leafy mountings and its big hammer like a parrot's head, did indeed look exceedingly Chinese, and once he had seen the Chinese in this, it was as though the Mandarin Fu Manchu was his old friend. There he was, in his high-necked brocade robe, bowing towards him against the background of a lacquered and flowery screen, and a great golden dragon on his robe wrapped his body around. The slanted green eyes, glittering as emeralds, caught his, and the slender hand, white and translucent as ivory, with its inch-long nail-shields, ushered him into the toadstool laboratory, pillared with the chunky stems like a squat cathedral, raftered with the fanning gills, and odorous with the distillations of the great Chinese scientist's many potions.

What the Hindu Kush was, under which the laboratory hummed and bubbled, George didn't know (nor probably did Uncle Fred), but there popped nevertheless into the boy's head the vision of a great slab of sandy red rock on which small villages perched above perilous fissures, under a sky echoing with thunderstorms. George felt he could sneeze when his uncle said 'pepper' and was going to, only then he felt in memory the salt of his tears, and swallowed hard. The mad Arab, fortunately, had concealed his unhinged face under the square-cut folds of his burnous, with a four-sided headdress very much like the black box itself, and an Amazon lady sat up abruptly, her kohled eyelids flapping languorously, an almond-shaped yellowish jewel like a tiger's eye staring threateningly from the middle of her forehead where it hung on a slender chain.

18

Now his uncle paused, and the pictures inside small George's head ceased, and he saw instead the vision his uncle had created with his glittering self, the small ancient pistol which he now held cocked and ready to fire pointing at the innocent black box on the small metal-legged table. *Bang!* a flash and a shower of sparks from the barrel, and the sides of the box fell down to reveal something very colourful that was unfolding and growing, and then, marvel of marvels, there shot up from the magic box a small tree of flashing tinfoil that broke the light into many colours and grew and grew with at its tip a bud which burst open into a creamy-white flower that slowly expanded and showed its centre full of big yellow anthers and a straight black pistil, and young George felt his little johnnie in his trousers grow too and become stiff and warm, and a thrill of pleasure went through his body which was as though he had been kissed all over. A strange coarse perfume came from the flower. The flashing light filled the room and dazzled him, and he really tasted tears now, and there was an aching lump in his throat, and he became embarrassed and turned away. It would be terrible to burst into tears here, among all the guests, people who would seize on the incident and turn it into a famous story against him, so that he would never be free of the shame among his friends. When he looked back at the table he saw a tawdry little Christmas tree, and there was no ivory flower growing at its tip.

Uncle Frederick had started on his next trick. 'You all know what a piggy-bank is, and you've heard of high finance, and you know about pennies from heaven, and you've heard that pigs might fly. But what about flying money, eh? You know my hat is full of rabbits, and the empty air is full of Christmas trees, and Dr Fu Manchu's pistol has the sparks of life in it that make the invisible visible. You know that there's everything everywhere, spirits in the pepper, doves under the tablecloths, red ribbons coiling everlastingly between your ears, and bouquets of flowers in the dining-room table itself, which was once an ancient tree that gave not only flowers but walnuts too, like those I cracked in my fingers after the Christmas pudding with the silver sixpences in it. Well, now you know that making Christmas pudding is a way of catching sixpences, just like flies on sticky flypaper, and sixpences are the flies of the financial world, but what are the doves of money, I ask you that? The white doves of money?' Sixpences were old money — a small coin worth two and a half new pence — but that was far into George's future. When his uncle said 'the doves of money' George thought of a wonderful bird made of the big white five-pound notes that he occasionally saw crinkling and crisping out of the wallets of grown-ups, with a beak from which gold sovereigns fell like big drops of honey.

'No, I'll tell you,' continued his uncle, flashing and glittering as he spoke, the little white stones set in his black cuff-links adding to the sparkling effect; his shirt-cuffs had eased themselves out of his jacket sleeves as his hands gesticulated his fast patter. It was way above the heads of the children there, but they loved him for it. 'They are the little silvery doves of money, no, they are the little round moon-beetles that I will catch for you, yes, the half-crowns!' There was a gasp from the children, who found half-crowns a very sizeable denomination: they were a coin worth an eighth of a pound, and a very generous week's pocket-money each one. 'Look at this drum of tin,' said Uncle, picking up another of his empty tins, this one open at the top, painted red, but deep and silvery inside as he tapped it with his little black wand with the white ends. 'Quite, quite empty, ladies and gentlemen, quite empty, but every cloud has a silvery lining, and these curtains are full of money on Tuesdays, watch ...' and he held the tin up to the heavy brown curtain, and as he held it there they all heard, quite distinctly, a coin drop into the empty tin. 'Look, there's another one here, they are crawling in the curtains like crabs of silver,' and another chink sounded in the tin, and the money scoured around inside and rattled as he shook it. 'It must be because there's a full moon this Christmas Tuesday, children, I mean, distinguished guests, look, I open the curtain slightly and there the moon is shining high, and I raise my drum to the moon and listen ...' There was a stream of money coming from the tiny, hard, icy full moon that swam beyond the curtains, evidently, for they all heard a succession of coins drop upon the other money in the tin. 'Here we are, let's look at the money-birds, the half-crowns with. wings that the moon has sent down to us like pollen that is made of shiny silver and has the King's head on it ...' He up-ended his tin and half-crowns poured out on the black velvet top of his little table.

'You've heard the expression "made of money", now let's see whether it's true of anybody here.' Uncle Fred passed his tin under the faces of the children in the front row, and from each chin or nose he elicited the *chunk* of a coin falling. 'Young George, you're a promising lad, what's your head full of, then? Dreams? Can we turn dreams into hard cash? Let's see.' And from George's nose, apparently, flowed a stream of half-crowns, as though he were the moon itself, and the moon was made of money,

21

and it had all come to George. Small George Pfoundes laughed up into his uncle's face that laughed down to him, and shook his head hard. 'No more, no more!' He was laughing so much, and as he shook his head he heard the rattle there of half-crowns forming again and again, like flowers of money budding inside his skull.

* * *

The consulting-room rustled with the sleepy echoes of the Oscilloscope giving back the sounds of their clothes, orchestrated for hypnosis. Dr Pfoundes always spoke to his patients as Uncle Fred, or as Fred's sister, Pfoundes' mother, or as the retired policeman who had been a soldier, and told the children bloody stories of the Great War, sitting in his cottage garden at the end of the street — all hypnotists in their way, though none so great as Uncle Fred. The three screens were idling, their colours like oil on water streaming by, with occasionally a falling-leaf shape to go with the rustle of cloth. The blind man, of course, was not aware of these pictures, but Pfoundes' voice describing the progress of their mysteries combined with the Oscilloscope's gentle auditory improvisations had been enough to put him into a medium-deep trance, and cataleptic phenomena were already developing. These are used as tests for the deeper states of hypnosis, in which the most remarkable work can be done: on command an arm grows as stiff as a steel bar, or a leg will remain straight out as if supported by a footstool, if the patient is told there is a footstool there.

Pfoundes now speaks as Uncle Fred, to his blind audience of one. 'Now, laddie, you are in the Garden

22

of Eden. You are mere soil in the Garden of Eden. I am the Lord God. You are relaxed, so deeply relaxed, clay in a great soggy warm heap under the sun. Here I am, the Lord God, walking in my garden in the evening, and I've got an itchy skin, like a horse or a deer has an itchy skin in the autumn, when the hair gets all dry, the pelt is dusty, the reddish-brown pelt of the Lord God, and my antlers are full-grown, the antlers of the Lord God.' The harmonics of the Oscilloscope gave a cathedral air to his words, save for a swishing in the background as if the cathedral were set with open doors in a windy savannah.

'The Lord God feels sexy, and he wants to bring life into his skin. He is alone, except for the animals he has created, animals like himself, herds of deer, or big-eared elephants.' There are fragments of trumpeting from the speakers, and a glimpse of grey skin in close-up, running away on the screens, a splash there like a herd charging through a waterfall. 'The Lord God sees this nice patch of clayey earth and he wants to do what the deer do, wallow in it. So he rears up on his hind legs and his great whanger comes out of its sheath and he pisses on you, laddie. You are privileged to feel the warm piss of God Almighty soaking into you with its life from beyond the stars!' Dr Pfoundes has a small glass dropper in his hand filled with saline solution; with deliberation he lets a drop fall on his patient's forehead and run down his cheek; another drop between his fingers. 'There! you can feel that glorious fluid like beer and wine — for God's piss is pure spirit to us, you know — running all over your skin and bringing you to life, intoxicating you with life!

'And now there is a further inestimable privilege for you, my lad, and that is that God having got you

23

all spirituous and nicely soft, he is going to wallow in you.' Now, without touching the skin, Pfoundes makes careful passes with his hands down over the blind man's forehead, over his chest and the front of his clothes, down below his waist to his groin, where he is gratified to see a responsive lump is growing. It is the case that men are always sexually excited during REM or dreaming sleep; nor can hypnosis be truly efficacious without sensuous images.

'How beautiful you smell; like good malt whisky; and it is your luxuriant slippery texture and his own good smell that God needs in this intercourse with himself, that is going to bring you to life. Feel God rolling and turning in you, wallowing in you, covering himself with you like a second skin.' Pfoundes' passes now, still without touching the skin, encompass the whole body. With mouth gaping the blind man writhes sensuously.

'Now the whole of you is on God's back, like an overcoat of warm clay, and on his front too for he has driven his chest and his penis in you as though the earth were a woman. What is this Lord God's name? I shall tell you one day, and you shall bear it as your special name as his only son out of the earth. Now God is levering the clay off him with the edge of his hoof, and as it comes away it bears, like a mould, his own image of you, and there you are, peeling off him in three great hollow pieces which God is fastening together. He puts his lips to the lips of the greeny-grey mould and blows into it, like a stiff balloon, which blushes delicately, and comes alive, no longer a hollow shell, but skin like that of a new-born babe, and its chest gently rises and falls, and it is full inside with the warm flesh of you created by God's breath. You lie naked, sleeping on the warm turf by

24

the empty black trench which is the space you occupied when you were no more than a long clod of earth. But now you are a man, a four-legged creature at least, lying on the ground, your eyes sealed, feeling the evening sun draw through you as it sinks and the coolness of the night comes on.' Pfoundes resumes his passes. 'But what is this? The animals are coming down to the water-hole to drink. The trench where you lay when you were clay is their water-hole. You are in their way. Here come the horses — quick! roll aside; you can feel their shadows cast on your skin.' Pfoundes has lit a medical examination light and directed it at one side of his patient's blind face; and in the light he is making shadow-animals with his fingers on the skin.

'Here come the delicate okapi, smelling of the grass they have been eating all day. Now they must quench their thirst. Lie still, or they will be startled and not be able to get past you in this narrow way. Now the lions come, slowly pacing; two magnificent males with tawny manes, and five females with their cubs tumbling after, and the rank smell of okapi torn to pieces on their breaths; now all the animals are friends, and drink together — until the mad bull elephant comes, who insists on drinking alone.'

Pfoundes' hands spread out to make the shape of an elephant's head with spreading ears, and he flaps the two hands towards the seeing skin of the blind man, and his voice rises high in apparent terror. 'Here he comes! the mad elephant! And all the animals are running from him. And you must run too because he will trample you into the ground and you will be no more than bloody footprints burst out of you soaking into the clay again, as if the Lord God had not been with you at all. Quick, get out of the way —

25

SEE WHERE HE COMES!' The blind patient had been tossing and turning as Pfoundes' voice, magnified by his invention, calls to him above a noise as of a hurricane forest, and at that last command suddenly he sits up in his chair and his eyes open wide and he looks through Pfoundes and he screams with terror.

The Oscilloscope takes his scream and gentles it back into the woodwind and into the calls of birds and the gentle plash of surf. The eyes are dark and staring, and follow the progress of something across the room and behind over his shoulder. Pfoundes quickly taps his patient's forehead with an outstretched finger. 'Quick, here I am. In the consulting-room. Here.' And he breathes into his face. 'That's me. My head is against the light and you can only see a shadow, but tell me how many fingers I am holding up.' Pfoundes lays three fingers against the man's forehead.

'Three fingers,' he faintly murmurs.

'That's right. Now I will move round into the light so you can see my face.' Pfoundes does not move, but his patient's head does, as though the doctor has moved round to his other side.

'There! Now you know me. You know this big chin, don't you? These rather greenish or hazel eyes? That's right. I have to wear this stiff collar in the office, you know. It's standard uniform for doctors. And this dark suit. But I do like a bit of colour in my tie, if I have to wear one — don't you? People like to see a doctor with a square head and dark hair neatly brushed and slicked back with some oil — you know, it looks so definite, and marks one with confidence — do you know me now, eh?'

'Oh yes, Dr Pfoundes. It is so good to see you after that terrible fright in the garden. I quite forgot myself! It was like a dream: and I had just woken from a dream in which I had been born from garden soil or clay ...' He is looking in the opposite direction to where the doctor is standing.

'Never mind about that now. You're here to see me about your eyes. There doesn't seem to be much wrong, but let's do a few tests. Just look at that colour chart on the wall, the one with the higgledy letters, just to your right. You see the letters: Z, T, Y, Q, G ... will you go on reading them?'

'X, C, H, U, V, now they're getting smaller, and I can just see little *w* and smaller *s*.'

'They're merging with the colours, aren't they? That yellow is particularly dazzling. Well, that seems all right. No pains? Very good.'

Pfoundes knows that this is a true blindness, and not a hysterical one. From a drawer he takes an ordinary ophthalmoscope.

He crosses over to where his patient is staring at the imagination of him, and fits himself into it, as it were.

'I just want you to look over my shoulder while I shine this little light into your eye.' Through the magnifying lens of the ophthalmoscope he can quite clearly see the deterioration of the retina. The ophthalmologist was, of course, absolutely right. There was no hope for the sight of this man. Had it been a hysterical blindness without optical deterioration, it would have been a comparatively simple matter to bring sight back under hypnosis, though the effect would not have been permanent without the discovery of the shock or the evasion that was making the man not wish to see. This case was, however, different; though it was a kind in which Dr Pfoundes had specialised with some success. He could indeed

27

bring sight to the blind — providing they had once seen and had a developed visual imagination — by making, in hypnosis, a link between the senses that were active in them, and this very same visual imagination. Then they would seem to see a touch on the skin, or see a face from the way the inside of the mouth smelt as he breathed on his patient, or the voice-vibrations outlining the body as they emerged from it. First it needed the successive shocks he had administered under hypnosis, which were designed to make the patient forget that he could not see, by causing him to dream very vivid visions awake. The effect of the hypnosis was to make the senses very excited, very sensitive, as they are, for instance, after making love satisfactorily; then the normal boundaries between them were thinned, and excitation would spread from one to the other, as if all the skin, for example, had become one great seeing eye. How light the clothes had to be on such a man; it would seem to him that his body was blinded by nets!

In this case, his treatment had gone very well indeed. His next action was to bring out of a cupboard a fat book, or rather, a number of substances bound together between boards, rather in the manner that people bind carpet-samples into a book. This was Pfoundes' catalogue of textures. In the excited state of the blind man's skin, he would immediately translate the various textures of substances into their visual equivalent. But not, Pfoundes hoped, in black and white. He hoped there would be enough visual imagination to make colours as well.

'Here, touch this.' He opened the book at a piece of dried crocodile skin.

'Oh, what a lovely piece of oak, cool and rough,' said the hypnotised man. 'I stand below and clasp the

28

trunk and I look upwards into the green canopy swinging with acorns. I crunch ripe acorns under my boots; I can see the little cups, empty, creamy inside with a white circle where the acorn went.' The Oscilloscope adds echoes: 'Now the wind is rising and I believe the oak is going to speak to me. It is a high wind, I can feel the trunk creaking and swaying under my hands.' Pfoundes now moves the oblong of skin to and fro under his patient's hands. 'Oh, oh, the leaves are threshing about like green crocodiles in a blue sea, green, green, the oak says green.'

Pfoundes now offers an oblong of blue silk. 'I reach up and touch the sky,' says the hypnotised man. 'I bring the sky down and it is the silky waist of a blue-clad lady with blue eyes I look deeply into as I dance.' Now Pfoundes opens his book at a steel mirror. 'Cool and smooth and glistening,' says the blind man; 'I walk with the lady past mirrors and I look over her shoulder into the glass and see I am dancing by myself . . .' 'Come closer to the mirror,' says Pfoundes. 'I scrutinise my face, it is a good job I'm fair since the stubble doesn't show at the end of the day, ah, Dr Pfoundes, you are here too, looking over my shoulder into the mirror with me.'

The next page in the book is a steel engraving of Dante on the threshold of Purgatory. 'How bright the stars are,' says the blind man, 'and there is a great ivy-clad oak at Virgil's right, and it is the first time I have seen Doré's picture in colour — and what colour! Those great tumbled leafheads on the left are olive-green in the starlight, and the water in the distance is a delicate steely blue, and that thunderstorm over the mouth of Hell is the most beautiful purple I have ever seen, despite what it must conceal.' Pfoundes has a small wooden box which he opens to show a double row of stoppered phials. He loosens the stopper of one of these slightly: it contains an aromatic substance of vile odour. 'Pah, pah, that is what is under the storm, those serried rows of punished faces all fixed by the necks to watch the Devil's anus, his kicking hooves, phew,' brushing his nose vigorously, 'what a fate for the friars, to watch the Devil fart'; this word is turned into a thunderous rumble by the Oscilloscope — 'and now the lightning darts down and strikes him in the guts, and the rain falls and cleanses him, and the damned faces watch, why,' he said, turning his face and his wide eyes up into Pfoundes' own, 'you are showing me moving pictures. This is very clever,' fingering the engraving, 'I have never seen illustrations that move three-dimensionally before.' He looks anxiously into Pfoundes' face. 'Your warmth is red, Doctor, I don't know how to express myself — have you given me a drug? — you have a skin like a lady that smells of perfumed soap, but your hair sounds dark. Listen to the blink of his eyes,' he mutters to himself, 'they are large, and the quills of stubble in his chin creak as he smiles at me.'

'You must wake up now,' said Pfoundes, 'you have seen enough for one day. Perhaps too much.'

'You wouldn't blind me again!' screams the blind man.

'No, no,' says Pfoundes, 'I only want you to wake up. You will remember all these dreams.'

'But I am not dreaming, I can see!' yells the blind man, getting up abruptly and pushing the doctor out of the way. 'I can see now. I don't need any more treatment. I grant that the world is still a little strange, but then I have been blind for twenty years. It is strange to me to see a bush in front of an open window

30

indoors,' he points to the desk, 'and it is strange too to be in a room whose walls rush in and out as I speak.' Pfoundes switches off the Oscilloscope. 'That is better. I can see the four walls plainly, and there is a fly walking on that cornice, a shrill black speck on the white. Your skin looks to me as if it is fuming; I can see your dark suit very plainly, and the echo of your shirt is very clean, but vapours are pouring from your cuffs, and your head seems to be composed of a pile of thick steam. Are you frightened? Let me get past to the door. I want to go out into the sunshine!' He walks rapidly towards a cupboard door and is about to open it, then pauses and gives a low shout. The echoes are apparently unsatisfactory, and the cupboard not deep enough to be an exit. He is uttering short mewing sounds now, his nostrils flared and twitching and his ears cocked. He walks rapidly and confidently towards the tall polished door he entered by. He pauses by a mirror, and seems puzzled for a moment, perhaps by its smooth gliding echo and cold smell, then with a chuckle utters a series of short coughs, peers into the glass adjusting his tie and smoothing an eyebrow with a wetted finger. He grasps the handle of the door saying, 'Goodbye, Dr Pfoundes. Please send me your bill,' and strides out. Pfoundes follows.

The nurse is sitting in the waiting-room plainly astonished by the confident figure that is just closing the outer door. Pfoundes stops a moment and gives her a professional smile and then, without unseemly haste, opens the front door and looks up and down the street.

Harley Street is not crowded. His patient is some distance away, weaving between the occasional pedestrians, who stare after him astonished at his chirping, mewing, coughing progress. Patients do not usually visit Harley Street in this state; it would be a bad advertisement for the cures. The erstwhile blind man looks about him. There is a light breeze blowing up the street. He has forgotten to take such outdoor phenomena into consideration: it will shift the odours and compress the echoes, making exact orientation difficult in this world of malleable objects. He steps off the kerb in front of a hurrying taxi. There is an awful bump and his body flies back on the pavement. Pfoundes can see his mouth an amazed black triangle in a blanched face.

On his knees by the dying man, Pfoundes bends his head to listen to his last words. 'A miracle, Doctor. Tell them all. The taxi was squashed up backwards by the breeze: I didn't realise it had reached me in advance of its appearance. The taxi leapt out of its appearance invisibly, and struck me down. My eyes saw, and didn't see. I should have heeded you, and I could have lived in a sighted world, but it was such a joy to understand that I was not dead like my eyes. My body gave the light. Now it's draining away, Doctor. I am blind again, and glad to die.' And the lids, which, as skin, had seen more than the dead eyes they contained, fell on an emptiness and a blackness like one of Uncle Fred's magic boxes.

* * *

Pfoundes remembers when he was able to hypnotise the animals. The quiet playground, and the biology master with the long sandy hair, a hen struggling under his arm. 'Draw a chalk-mark on the ground, George,' said his friend the master, 'and I'll show you how to hypnotise hens.' Thirteen-year-old

George did so, just a short line, about eighteen inches long, with the tall Scotsman looking on. 'That's the way to do it,' and holding the hen firmly he put it down on the tarmac, and turned its beak so that the poor bird was looking along the line, down in the pecking position. It fluttered a little, drew its wings in, and stayed where it was. 'That's hypnosis, George,' said his teacher; 'that hen would stay there until it starved. All it can see is the direction of that line, which has caught it by the pecking reflexes. That's what you could do to a human being, George Pfoundes, if you messed about hypnotising without proper training. If I ever catch you trying to hypnotise your friends again, I'll have you up in front of the headmaster with a full report. Now go to the library, look in Yapp's *Animal Physiology* and write me an essay on "Conditioning and Control". I want you to start with the processionary caterpillars that Fabre got to march endlessly round and round the rim of a flowerpot, poor creatures, as it was natural for them to form processions, and they couldn't help following each other; discuss Skinner's "religious reflex" and finish up with a bit on brainwashing.'

Pfoundes did, and that schoolboy essay grew into his first book, *Conscious Instinct and Self-Control,* which he published while he was still at Cambridge, and which eventually bought him a medical practice. Its theme was that indeed we are animals, and we are stuffed with instincts, which we attempt to deny, and this causes much distress and many illnesses. But we are also conscious beings, and if we uncover our deep instinctual responses and allow them to grow, we can enjoy them consciously, and become whole. It is a matter, he wrote, of discovering the 'True Will' and following it. He was aware that he was echoing

33

the writings of Aleister Crowley in using this term 'True Will': 'Do what thou wilt shall be the whole of the Law'; and 'Will under Law'. Pfoundes, however, used arguments from scientific research, and did not mention the word 'magick' once in this book. He wrote about simple hypnotic techniques, and the chapters that showed how a woman might consciously discover the way her organs developed and acted in preparation for and during childbirth, were widely used. His simple techniques allowed one to image the organs as if they were separate living creatures: to image them, converse with them in imagination, and relax them. It was reckoned that the chapter called 'Conversations with the Womb' had saved as much suffering as nitrous oxide. The being that spoke from the womb for many women was a beautiful horned male, to whom the book gave the name Dionysos.

The incidents that led to the schoolmaster's kindly reprimand were an offshoot of a school-children's game popular at the time. The idea was that your friend breathed rapidly in and out for a little while, and then took a big breath — but you clasped him round the chest with your two arms and stopped the full inhalation with all your force. The result was that your friend fell limp into your arms. There was nothing special about the uncon-sciousness: you were simply knocked out. But the kids got together to do this for dares. Once the grown-ups got wind of the game, it was strictly forbidden. At Pfoundes' school the MO got up one morning and gave his masturbation lecture with this dare-game substituted for the dreaded wanking. He warned the children that it would age them prema-turely, and might result in strokes and paralysis. In fact what happened was that an alkalosis and a sudden lowering of blood-pressure was produced which drew blood from the head. There might also have been a little shock-wave in the vascular system of the sort that is produced by a karate-blow on the carotid artery, so perhaps the MO was right.

* * *

What Pfoundes had found was twofold. First of all, and this was not an original discovery, he found that it was very pleasant doing this to little girls. Their dresses felt cool and their fronts were soft. The other thing, which was his discovery, was that if you held them while they were limp instead of dropping them to the ground, and whispered in their ear that they were to do something, likely as not they started doing that thing as soon as they came to. Pfoundes had filled the playground with little girls dancing in their light school uniforms, the skirts swirling, their eyes firmly closed, while his friends stood around at first guffawing and then reduced to silence by the strange floating blissful little automata. The tall Scotsman had come on the scene, and understood at once what had happened. 'Tell them to wake up,' he whispered urgently to small Pfoundes; 'call it out and stop them dancing.' Pfoundes did so, and the whirling rhythmic pretty dance of the girls faltered, and they shivered and came awake, rubbing their eyes. One of the girls burst into tears; the others did not seem to be affected by what had happened. They walked gingerly, for they were dizzy. A little girl called Alice went on dancing. She wore a white frock; she was out of uniform, being a junior prefect. Pfoundes walked over to her and tried to stop her.

35

She evaded his grasp, eyes closed, smiling. He ran behind her, talking to her: 'Why won't you wake up, Alice?' This, as it happens, is the correct procedure to follow if anybody is hypnotised and won't dehypnotise: you ask them why. 'I so want to dance with someone,' said Alice. Pfoundes, behaving beyond his years, took the girl in his arms. They danced half a dozen steps together, twirling twice, then the girl opened her eyes and shook out her hair. 'That was nice, George,' she said.

Pfoundes remembers when he was able to hypnotise the animals. He was an undergraduate, and he had just sat his finals in the Summer term, and he was panic-stricken. It was pride: he had published his book; it was under an assumed name in this, the first edition, but he thought how radically silly it would be if he failed his exams having written *Conscious Instinct and Self-Control*. It was all very well to argue, as he did, that there was nothing instinctual about sitting for examinations: it was an artificial rite of passage through and through. But of course he needed his medical degree if he was to go on. Where was his Self-Control? He had used hypnotic methods: he had hypnotised himself for his revision, and he had hypnotised himself for the exam itself, and had written in a light trance: but the concomitant of this was that he could not remember exactly what he had done *in his own person*. It had seemed to him that another personality, a larger one, one that was as familiar with the contents of the medical books as the remote authors themselves, and so did not need to read in the ordinary fashion, line by line, had taken over — but now he was *not* that person, he was George Pfoundes, and George Pfoundes was a slow stick. It was that other person he wished to be — if he could stand the pace of that flashing-devouring mind he thought he experienced. But did he, or was it all self-deception? The results would tell him, perhaps sooner than he wanted, because he had never felt such exhilaration as when he was in contact with this apparently greater self, who knew medicine like a master. This could be a madness, a nervous break-down — indeed, hypnosis was a bit like madness, a calm madness deliberately courted.

At any rate, he was exhausted, as though this new mind he had contacted used up bodily energy at a greater rate than usual; or perhaps as though Pfoundes could not yet accept the return of mental energy that his other self gave: not yet, they were not yet one (granting that the whole experience was not a delusion). Pfoundes wanted to get away. The die was cast, as they say; he could do nothing; when he returned to London he would know his professional fate. Not only that, he would know if he had been mad.

He chose the Scillies, the cluster of islands off Land's End, in Cornwall. Nobody could get further away than that. Moreover, he would book his hotel on the smallest of the inhabited islands: Tresco, the civilised Scilly, where, in an enlightened feudal experiment, one Augustus Smith had taken the islanders that he had found dining on seaweed and limpet broth, and formed them into work-forces to build him a house, and to plant belts of Monterey pines that had turned the island from a windswept rock on which its human inhabitants camped huddled in cottages like the armoured limpets themselves, to a smiling fertile Fortunate Isle, carefree, green, full of daffodil fields.

The journey was horrible. First the steam-train

from London to Penzance; by express, but still a nine-hour journey in those days. Then an overnight stay in the opulent and comfortable Queen's Hotel, with its hall full of oil paintings and drawings by quite distinguished local artists, its wide staircase and its balconied bedrooms. Early rise for the *Tresconian*, the island boat that would take its passengers out along the rocky coast beyond Land's End to the Scilly Islands themselves, which jutted in the sea there like drowned peaks of a sunken land: Lyonesse, so the legends went. These were the Isles of the Dead, where Stone Age man had buried his chieftains, and this accounted for the wealth of ancient tumuli and stones. Perhaps it also accounted for 'Scilly', which can mean 'holy' as in German *selig*.

The sea-voyage was then famous for its bumpiness. In the shelter of the cliffs of south-west Cornwall the passage was smooth, even majestic: the landlubber swaggered, and smoked brave cigarettes. Once out of this shelter, the sea swell, even if there was not an actual gale, was large and oily, and one sought the spine of the deck for least roll, and avoided the hatches, since the oily smell rising from them reinforced the metaphor by giving the glutinous roll and toss of the sea an olfactory dimension. The passengers huddled, G. F. Pfoundes among them. Once on the swift current that flowed between the islands, the tidal current, matters were easier, but Pfoundes was unable to watch the scrolling glide of the seabird, since it made the ship's planks far too unstable. He was at his best with his eye firmly fixed on the furthest horizon, which did not roll much in comparison with the nearer world.

The green-faced passengers staggered off the *Tresconian*, which had docked at St Mary's, under the gaze of unsympathetic locals, who regarded it as decent sport to watch the new arrivals counterfeiting sprightly walks, looking around them alertly, like people glad to be on holiday and not regretting it one bit. Pfoundes dissembled with the best of them, but then realised that he still had another journey. 'Tresco Hotel, sir?' A blue-jerseyed figure tipped its white cap, and soon he was on the sea again, holding himself in, unwilling to spill himself in any further retching, this time in an open launch, the blue-jerseyed navigator with the white cap skimming him over the white-capped blue depths.

This journey was not too bad as the fresh air blowing on his face soothed his stomach, kept his mind away from it. He realised that this was the essence of a kind of hypnotism — strange that he had not thought of applying hypnotic methods to counteract motion-sickness. But the air on his face was a caress, a massage, a hypnotic pass, a long pass lasting the whole journey through which his body travelled, and it produced in him a concentration on himself as a face without a stomach: it reduced the irrelevant sensory input from below and concentrated his spirit on a calm and fortified expression rather than a churning, over-sensitive and over-animal part of him. He cut the air like a figure-head or the calm prow of a ship. Which did not prevent him from throwing up all over his overcoat as the boat took an unexpected curve against the slapping small waves and rocked like a nursery horse.

He wiped at himself with his handkerchief. It was just mucus with a little bile, and he felt much better for it. A leathery hand took his and helped him step ashore. On the little stone jetty he looked around him.

The sky was overcast. He saw black rocks dotting a smooth sea that ran with the tide and shone brighter than the sky. It was as though a mountainous district had been flooded, and only the peaks showed their tips above the still-active flood. What villages, what flocks, lay drowned below the speeding water? He walked the narrow path between bushes of green succulents with strange crimson flowers. He was on a driveway, and a large man in a blue shirt shook him by the hand and welcomed him to the hotel.

The bed in his room still rocked. After a while he got up, despairing of rest, and put on his heavy shoes for a walk. Outside it was still overcast, and looked like rain. He had noticed a deeply-brackened path that looked attractive on his walk from the boat. He would take this and see where it went. On his right he passed great tall bushes surrounding a clearing in which a thick dark tree stood. 'Colonel Tree' came into his mind; it looked so strong and tall, with a shako of leaves, and branches like brandishing green swords in the slight wind. The shrubbery hissed. The path went on between the brackened heath and he had to pass a narrow opening in a hedge, guarded by two peeled-white posts. In front of him were massive bluffs of greenery rising to a tall hill or plateau that must be the centre of the northern part of the island, he thought. On his right, smoke was coming from a rubbish dump that was covered with gulls like a white tablecloth that lifted slightly as he passed, and then resettled. The path, he could see, drew a line along the curve of a small bay where the bracken was really quite tall, up to his shoulder, and damp. His trousers were by now quite soaked.

He heard a strange abrupt *kirrick-kirrick* above his

head, and ducked as something white and black plummeted from the sky and blurred past his face. He raised his arm across his eyes and looked about him. The sky was clear, so far as he could see, below the cloud canopy, which was whitey-grey with patches of angry purple. Then *kirrick-kirrick* came again with a resonance that was unfamiliar to him, rather like a cross between a note on the piano and a glass breaking, a rifle-shot: a strange combination of explosion and whistle. The rush came by his head again and he saw the tern with its black cap and forked tail swoop round and take position for another dive at his head. Other birds of the same kind were gathering in the sky, randomly passing and dipping; the effect was gripping, and he stared up at them until he realised that his eyes might be just the target they required, and they might be capable of manoeuvring him like this into exposing them. He thought of the serpent hypnotising its victim; he thought of George Pfoundes hypnotising his school-fellows. He wished he had not come to Tresco; or at least that he had rested from the sea before meeting this new threat, coloured black and white like the depressing clouds.

Another *kirrick-kirrick* and he fell to his knees between the tall bracken as the bird swept at him almost chest-high and missed his head at the last moment. What had he done to deserve this attack? Was he near the eggs somehow? Had he taken the wrong path? Were there warning notices he had not seen that these terns — which he knew were a very rare bird — were dangerous at nesting time? He came, half-running now, into a more open space, and looked wildly about him, thinking that perhaps he might be best protected if he burrowed among the

41

bracken stalks with his jersey over his head, wondering whether he would have to crawl back to civilisation and the hotel through the bracken, head down, humiliated by birds. Two birds were hunting him now, from opposite directions, at the same time; *kirrick-kirrick* and a great swish of feathers held him still for a moment before his stumbling run took him to the lee of a small boulder that was embedded in the turf.

He leant against the rough granite, that was slightly luminous in this light from the mica reflections in its surface. He enjoyed the stability of the rock, and was very glad to have its protection at his back. Its calm and cool pressure as he leant against it soothed him, and reduced his panic so he was able to think. The terns still weaved their way over his head in the space above the small bay, and he could not distinguish which were the two sentries. Perhaps they were all massing for an attack. They sounded their *kirrick-kirrick* sound as they flew, but without the plangency of the attacking cry, the scream of the dive-bomber broken into attacking notes like its machine-gun bullets. It really was a most disturbing cry, he thought, and was no doubt meant to paralyse its victims, just as a human cry on the right note at the right moment could hold a person still. He had seen a famous doctor use a 'confusional' technique of inducing a trance by talking vivid nonsense very rapidly, and then calling out suddenly, *'Sleep!'* whereupon the patient fell into a deep trance. A perfume seemed to come into the air from the bracken and the stone as this idea came into his mind, like a new dimension to the scene. He realised that the boat had made him very upset, and he had become depressed. The overcast sky and the unfamiliar

42

place had shrunk in his mind, or, rather, his responses to it had shrunk, and a depression had stolen on him unawares. He had been thinking of the path, and the wonderful greenery, and the sea and the birds as things to be walked through, to take a healthy tramp through for the benefit of his own bodily health, not as parts of a complex organism that were to be approached with some courtesy, in some depth, and tentatively. With this realisation, the fear went too, and the massing of the birds and their flight was no longer like the menacing weaving of a serpent's head, but more like the air made visible by its creatures' joy in it, as they stepped with their wings from airstream to airstream. He thought: this came on me as I relaxed against this stone. Where had the next attack gone? They seemed to mind me when I was walking alone. Perhaps it was my depression they smelt, or they saw me like a crackling fire of contrary human currents come walking near their nests; perhaps I was giving off distressed sub-sonics, perhaps the life in me was crying, 'Destroy, destroy.' Now this stone is my companion, they do not mind me. There are more birds, but perhaps they are coming to look at this man companion to a stone, whose contrary electricities that felt so destructive are draining away into the ground, where all things are remade. I think that my skin now looks to them more like the calm mirror of that stone, and that when I was depressed their flight raised little tracks or weals of fire, angry inflammations of electricity on my skin so that I looked like a red fire of scales, or like a serpent ready to eat their eggs. Now, in my calm, I look like this stone, whose clever grain of feldspars and quartz reflects the currents of the air and water they are gliding on in a different, calmer sense, like a mirror or

a camera, or the retina of a great earth-eye storing
their movements reflected deep in the tiny flakes of
transparent mineral, like the compound eye of an
insect. Perhaps this is their marker, and their touch-
stone. At this thought, a tern swooped down again,
but without the attacking cry. Pfoundes did not
flinch, as he had before, and he let the jersey that
he had torn off and wrapped round his fist in case
he were attacked again drop silently to the ground.
He let himself become filled with thoughts of the
mutuality of the rock and the bracken and the birds,
the sea and the air, and grew more greatly relaxed.
The scene around him grew more solid and real to
him with this participation in it. The tern that had
swooped landed on the rock at his left hand. Its eyes
were imperially fierce, with a deep black centre, and
a golden iris like carefully folded gold foil. The beak
like a sharp thorn was tipped with yellow. It paced
the small space on the rock where his hand rested,
and without a break in its stride stood on his hand.
Another bird landed on his right shoulder, and
craned its head round to look in his face. He felt
strong claws in his hair and birds walked about his
feet. Another tern settled on the knuckles of his
right hand, and two more on his extended left arm.
They were silent, and Pfoundes waited for whatever
might come; he was as real and vivid to himself as
that tern's feathers of misty grey were, and they
were like organs of his body, like feathered masks
that he was wearing, but then, were they not wearing
him, and the rock and the grass wearing them all?
Suddenly all the wings raised and flapped together,
and had anyone been watching they would have
seen an appearance like a tall man standing in white
flames that covered him. Then the birds launched

themselves in the air, and left him. As he walked back along the path, he saw his companions of the island saluting far above.

* * *

What was not hypnotism? he wondered. All the magic in his life was rooted in what was natural, and truly magic. When he hung in his mother's belly he was at one with his environment, as he was one when the angry seabirds accepted him. When he was clothed in their living feathers and among the wings flapping like a furnace-draft, he had been sexually excited, his penis had risen, and it amused him to think that, had he been unclothed, a tern might have perched on it quite naturally as a useful projection, or have masturbated him with its soft breast-feathers or its flapping wings. In sleep and dreaming all people are sexually excited, while they encounter the internal bodily experiences which are the substance of the dream; he saw it in his patients, too, whom he could, and did, make dream by touching them. It was to make the body speak in images that he did this. The dreams of the child in the womb: were these any different from the formative processes that were making the baby grow in harmony with the genetic code that was implanted in it? Were dreams this DNA code made visible? Did hypnosis work by returning a person to this reverie of growth and the fulfilling of natural possibilities? What a great hypnotist this Science is!

Then, when he was born, his mother de-hypnotised him, with the assistance of the presiding doctor. He was thrust out of his symbiosis into a world of light and dark, harshness and gentleness, right and wrong. But he knew that, to grow properly, that kind of

45

'reality' was not all there was. Periodically his mother must 'rehypnotise' him into symbiosis. What a shame that this word 'hypnotise' implied the imposing of a falsehood on a person! There was no falsehood imposed when his mother distracted him with her glittering button-box into calm and conscious content, into an involvement with the play of light in transparent, diamond-like buttons, its chopping up into the little round mirror-segments called 'sequins', its undulation within the surface of an iridescent mother-of-pearl button, like eels twisting underneath a sea-surface, or seabirds flying in strange weaving patterns. One would lose oneself there, and find oneself, and grow to be oneself in such timeless distractions. Pfoundes has seen a whirling wheel driven by motors in the consulting-room of a fellow hypnotist; it had mother-of-pearl facings and a polarised light-source that emphasised the twisting patterns. It would so fill the mind with its simple patterns unfurling into endless possibilities, that the hypnotist's basic commands would be understood by the patient as the exact possibilities that they were. 'You will feel no desire to smoke cigarettes . . . They are so boring, cigarettes, why trouble to light that one, after all they make you cough, and a cough is so unpleasant, and the smell is not really socially acceptable, so why light up? It is simpler, surely, not to burn this weed, not fill your lungs with this harsh feeling, but to enjoy the gentle air vibrant with sunlight, or the night air full of the sound of waters and the tang of moonlight, to open yourself to the natural air rather than to impose this stain on it . . .' And indeed, why not, all that he said is true, and I can see it in the unfurling corridors of my mind, and the possibilities open out just like that light twirling in that revolving button; and as my mother says to me as I am unpacking her button-box and am looking at that large dark mirror that once fastened her day-suit across her breast, 'Ah, you will be a great man, Georgie, you are afraid of nothing! All you have to do is to keep going and be afraid of nobody's opinion.' Then as the light unwinds in this button between my mother's fingers I can see quite plainly how this is true, and how George Frederick Pfoundes, the great hypnotist in his consulting-room with its crazy-coloured walls, beckons to me down the long corridor of days and nights, in his crazy-coloured tie, in his suit glittering with just such large dark buttons, double-breasted as is proper.

Shortly after the incident with the birds, Pfoundes wondered whether he could change the smell of his skin so as to attract ladies. He was adept at the kind of hypnotic procedures that controlled these normally involuntary signals or emissions of information. He could quite easily throw himself into a light trance by simple relaxation and concentration on his breathing. He would relax from the crown of the head downward, imagining that a soothing warmth was being projected into his skin, so that it covered his head like a hat. Then the hat would let down veils over his face that warmed it and soothed it, and it would clothe him in a gradually extending shirt-and-trousers that were made of this same pink-coloured, warm, soothing radiation. It was as if, in his imagination, he was clothed in his living birth-membranes. Then he would find that his breathing had slowed, become light and regular. He would deliberately feel his breath entering his nostrils and travelling down into his lungs, and, as it were, lighting them up with fresh oxygen, that was turning his warm blood bright

47

red. He would then usually feel that his hands were getting larger, and tingling, and that as a baby in the womb or like a dirigible balloon he was floating on a stalk. He would allow this impression to grow, until he was quite sure that the stalk entered him at his navel, and he would now pretend that every time he breathed out he did so in this region of his belly, and that it would glow like the red roses of coals through which a current of air is blown.

Having felt these sensations, which he knew any-body could feel — they were natural and practice is all that is required — he was in control, he knew. By an act of imagination that was curiously dual, he could now make himself break into a slick silvery sweat. The imagination was dual because he had to do two things at once. To imagine that he was very hot, and sweating, or fearful and sweating (the best image was to phantasise that he was in Africa and facing a charging lioness with a gun that he was hastily reload-ing) — that was the first degree of imagining. The second was that he could simply let the water through the skin, that he could make the skin full of pores through which the water poured (the *clang* associa-tion was oddly helpful). And it did. He had done it at parties, to his hostess's command.

Or he could make himself blush, fierily. Or he could blanch his face into a terrible mask of fear with black-circled eyes, like an actor in a German expressionist film, such as *The Cabinet of Dr Caligari*. 'Do Caligari' was the cry, and 'You should have been an actor!' What was an actor but a man who had acquired this ability to hypnotise himself into a part? Pfoundes asked himself. For a lover's amuse-ment he would write words on his own chest: this was a hypnotic phenomenon akin to the medieval

48

miracle of the 'stigmata' in which a saint would so identify himself with the sufferings of Christ that the five wounds would open on his body, and bleed regularly in time to devotions. All he needed to do was to trace his finger over the flesh when he was in this relaxed and concentrated state, and shortly afterwards the writing would come up in raised livid weals. 'I love you I bleed for you' had won him deep bedward conquests by appearing suddenly on his chest after he had taken his shirt off. The conquests were very worthwhile, as it was in this state that Pfoundes made love, always; his skin was infinitely deep and sensitive, infinitely responsive to that of his partner, inside and outside. He would follow her orgasms with his own responsive climaxes: 'ghost-orgasms' they were, avoiding the masculine sudden explosion and refractory period after orgasm which can so discontent a women who has just entered her own staircase experience in which climax can follow climax without a refractory period; until he was sure that he was ready for his deepest response, and she also was ready to finish. Thus, by 'hypnosis' he was able to travel with the woman as equal multi-orgasmic partner; and always, before and after, his skin gave off those harmonies of sensation which became pictures, smells, chords of music as they sank further and further into unity. His invention, the Pfoundes Oscilloscope, was a model of these experiences, to induce this kind of happening in his patients with whom the commitment to physical intimacy was impossible.

After the episode with the Tresco terns, he began to vary his repertory a little. Scientific work on what were called 'external chemical messengers' had just appeared. Later, these substances were called 'pheromones', meaning 'external hormones', because they were chemical substances, given off into the air by the lungs and skin and the various bodily apertures, which had an effect on the physiology of the organism that breathed them comparable to that of the *internal* chemical messengers that circulated in the blood in amazingly minute amounts to control most of the vital functions of growth and reproduction. Certain animals and plants, it was found, gave out these pheromones as a kind of body-language of powerful effective words and declarations, like spells. Some were love-potions: it had been shown that the pheromones of the rat would cause the male animal to go crazy for love, and stimulate his enormous and incessant potency. Typically of science, pheromones that inhibit sexuality had been discovered in human vaginal secretions. These occurred after the mid-cycle ovulation in fertile women: as though the womb was saying 'I've got an ovum here; you may have impregnated me; do not disturb the possibility of my child growing with any further importunities.' But it was also hypothesised that other substances brought the male on in an earlier part of the cycle; and that during sexual excitement these substances might be given off by both sexes. The menstruation pheromone was thought to be so powerful sexually that it would cow most men; this accounted, in the opinion of this researcher, for the conventional taboo on sex at the period.

Pfoundes, in his relaxed, concentrated state, imagined himself menstruating. He imagined that he had gone without sleep for several nights. He felt bloated, restless, irritable, his eyes gritty. Then, with a strange delight, the blood came. Now he felt proud, as though he were wearing a mark of identity

50

or a sigil of magic. He first tried this at the Club, deeply ensconced in one of the ancient leather armchairs in the reading-room. It was not his fancy, but there really was a rustling of newspapers and a restlessness spread. Members left. The club secretary came in, looked round suspiciously, sniffed, and called for a club servant. 'I wonder if he is telling him that he must enforce the no-ladies rule' — shaky finances had compelled the Club to admit distinguished women members upon election, but they were not allowed in the reading-room or the corridor leading to it and the gentlemen's lavatory and barbershop. Occasionally one did stray in this direction, but she was usually diverted from her course before any damage was done.

Pfoundes himself left the room, wondering whether he imagined the wake of restlessness he left behind him. Now he got a taxi to Lady Patricia's party in Knightsbridge; he would act as a woman in his imagination, and take his menstruation with him. He rang and Patricia's husband, Arthur, who had no title other than 'Pat's husband', opened the door, and looked rather vaguely at him and around him, as though he *saw* he was alone, but was not convinced that he was unaccompanied. 'Come in, George! Nice to see you. On your own tonight? Prowling? What else is a party for?' and he let him in.

Much later somebody said 'Do Caligari.' 'I'd rather not,' said Pfoundes. 'Awww' went everyone. So Pfoundes did Caligari. A blonde girl in a long silver dress arranged a spotlight, and Pfoundes stuck his head through the curtains of an alcove. The other lights were switched off. Pfoundes' rather square face with its big clean-shaven chin and slick black eyebrows and hair went very still. His watchers

51

went still too. There was a spurt of a giggle, but everybody went *hush* and the giggler stopped. The very still face hanging in the curtained alcove suddenly went bright scarlet, then it streamed with sweat through the scarlet as though it had become dashed with rain, then the blood drained away from it and it was chalk-white with deep black circles round the eyes, and sweat dripped off the large chin; then swiftly the mouth opened as if to roar silently and the eyes crossed as a man's head that was also a lion's head roared silently down upon them, and then the nose went beaky and the eyes hooded and a feeling of ancient time crept across the face as though the giant land-turtle on which the whole world rested had come into the room, then the face smoothed out and the eyes became large and clear and there seemed to be no teeth, for the lips parted and a bubble of saliva blew between the gums and they saw a great baby's head hanging at a man's height, then the lips went very thin and straight and the nose seemed to run into the upper lip and the eyes glittered and it licked its tongue so swiftly that you could not swear that it was not forked, and then the countenance smoothed again and appeared to become very leathery and wrinkled in the spotlight and the grease on the hair touched the light and silvered it so that they were looking at the serene white-haired face of a very holy man, suspended like an apparition in a dream. Arthur sniffed a little; his throat was unaccountably husky and his eyes swam with tears at the beauty of this face — which then composed itself around a large clean-shaven chin and walked through the curtains as the countenance set squarely on the dark double-breasted shoulders of the young doctor of hypnosis, George Pfoundes, who smiled at

52

them cheerfully, picked up his glass, and sat down. There was a subdued rustle of applause and somebody started up the record-player again.

Lady Patricia waddled over to the seated Pfoundes. She was a small plump woman with very large hips who had been treated by Pfoundes for painless childbirth: one of his first patients and almost the foundation of his practice.

'I want post-hypnotic suggestion for relaxation when I have this child,' Patricia had said, very stout with her second son.

'My dear lady,' said Pfoundes, with his professional air, just avoiding the honorific address, 'with hips like that why do you need hypnosis?'

'My Rupert nearly killed me. I hadn't the faintest idea what was happening, and I hated gas — just like the dentist.'

'Do you know what is happening now?'

'I think so . . .'

'Then. relax, and look at the little spot of light in the black card, and feel your eyes grow heavy, so heavy . . .'

She was a good subject, and Pfoundes was able to make her feel, inwardly, proprioceptively (the technical term), the child in her womb, and taught her to converse with it in her imagination, and give it all the qualities she wished to see in her son; and he showed her how to feel the birth-passage, and told her what to expect in labour. He was not present at the birth, but the accoucheur told him he had never seen an easier delivery, nor a quieter baby. Pfoundes had asked her whether she was pleased with the child, and she replied that she certainly was, but could Pfoundes do anything for Arthur, who was a bit boring? Pfoundes took this as a jest;

53

Lady Patricia half hoped that Pfoundes' skill could brighten Arthur up a bit, and was always bringing the subject up. Pfoundes thought that if he attempted such a treatment, he would lose both friends. He told Patricia to be content with the child, and to bring it to him just before it was ready to start school, and he would see that her son learnt a way to still himself against all that a school could do to diminish a child's natural abilities.

Now Patricia slapped him on the back and told him that he had given a wonderful performance. She said that she had once been to a spiritualist seance where the spirits materialised faces, hanging in the air outside the circle, or replacing the medium's face with their ectoplasmic masks. 'Is this how they do it?' she asked.

Pfoundes replied that mediumistic trances were very similar to his own practice, but that didn't make the seance a fake, since he supposed that the information the spirits gave was at least as useful as the self-knowledge he enabled his patients to discover.

'Were they really spirits, then?'

'So much happens when you open up the channel to the dark areas of the brain, the ones we use in dreaming; who can say what entities and principles are perceived in this way? I keep an open mind. Mediums have very strong natural ability, whereas much of mine was learnt for medical purposes. One day, perhaps, I will be privileged to become a medium.'

'You're teasing me, George,' said Patricia, easing a little closer to him. 'You have such an air tonight that I could think you were Old Nick himself, guardian of the dead!'

Pfoundes was puzzled by this; such an aura would not necessarily be professionally sound, he thought;

then he remembered that in his imagination he was still menstruating, and no doubt his skin was giving off the appropriate pheromones. Perhaps this had helped his performance; had Patricia asked him whether he had hypnotised them, or only himself, he would not have known how to answer.

'George — you smell like a butcher, your sweat smells like a butcher's shop, George; I want, I want . . .'"

'Patricia, my love, I'm very fond of you, as you and Arthur . . .' but he was saved any further conventional excuses by a new voice.

'Old Nick, eh? The zig-zagger, the man of many faces. Do you ever take your shoes off, Dr Pfoundes, are they specially blocked to take hooves?'

The speaker was a remarkably beautiful woman Pfoundes had noticed earlier, through the curtain, weighing up his audience as was his custom, preparing to remove them one by one from his imagination, so that only the skin of his face remained as inhabitant of the room. He had seen this woman, and had been a little startled to see that as she settled herself on the carpet cross-legged, she had tilted her eyes up into her lids, and this produced a flash of white. This interested him in two ways: it was unexpected in a good-looking woman as, if it were a habit, it would repel most people; it was also a sign that she was an unusually good hypnotic subject, if she could roll her eyes up like this while she was closing them. After his 'act' he noticed that she was one of the three people who had wept at the face of the 'guru' that he had put on by imagining a 'holy person' alone but in every fibre connected with all living things.

'No, I'm sorry — that sounds rude. I was so impressed by your performance, not the least because I've seen it before.'

55

Pfoundes felt a slight pique at this; so far as he knew, it was unique.

'Do you mean at a spiritualist seance?'

'Not exactly, Dr Pfoundes. It was the *Lindwurm*.'

He wondered whether she were Swedish, though she was very dark, since she pronounced this word with a curious accent, very slow on the second syllable, with the hint of a hiss in the voice. After she had spoken, she kept her eyes on him, as though she had said a password, and was expecting him to respond.

'I'm afraid that I don't know that name. You wouldn't mean Dr Lindstrom, by any chance? He is an excellent hypnotist.'

'No *sir*,' she said. 'I see we speak different languages, though we may be discussing the same matters.'

'Excuse *me*,' said Lady Patricia, with a false smile. She got up. 'Where's Arthur?' she said, 'I must find Arthur. He really ought to come and see you, George, he's been like he is long enough. I'll go and find him and get him to promise while he's had a few.' She waddled off.

'What matters?' asked Pfoundes. He thought he was prepared to go to bed with this lady, who looked like the find of the season. But she also sounded a little dotty, and unless it was a kind of dottiness he was already familiar with, he didn't feel inclined to take on a patient when he needed a holiday.

'I don't know what you will think of this,' she replied, 'but I must use the language I know. It may sound nuts to you, but please believe it is only a way of trying to understand an experienced reality. After all, what you just did was pretty remarkable.'

'That's kind, but it is only a party-trick.'

'I have never seen a good party-trick that didn't have an inner meaning for those who were ready for it; and those who weren't would enjoy and remember what the conjurer did, until they were ready to make use of it. It is as though such people as yourself give the dream flesh. This is why I asked you whether you had hooves.'

'Not to my knowledge, ever,' said Pfoundes; 'would you like to look?'

He offered her a highly-polished patent-leather pump, which to his surprise the lady accepted. She slowly drew off his shoe. He looked at his foot, the left one. Under the black silk sock it looked oddly shaped, like a club foot. She crooked her knuckle and knocked against it. It made a bony sound. He quickly reached down and grasped it: it was warm and flexible like it normally was, like any other foot. He took his hand away and looked at his foot again. It was the familiar shape and size. He looked at the lady. She laughed. He laughed.

'What does that mean?'

'What does what mean?'

'My foot . . .'

'Well, some people enjoy having their shoes taken off by kind strangers. It's relaxing.'

'A bit too relaxing.'

'That from you — I thought the basis of hypnosis was relaxation.'

'I'm sorry, I was caught unawares.'

'That is how destiny appears, they say. Suddenly — the voice breaks and he knows he is a man. Maybe he has a dream before this, though.'

'I thought my foot had changed.'

'Well, what does that mean?'

'What I knew already, that the hypnotist is the

57

most suggestible man of them all.'

'And where I come from, we honour such men.'

'Where do you come from, Miss . . .?'

'Actually, my name is Lindqvist.'

'Do you use that as a first name?'

'Only when I want to seduce a man. It is a little — formal — as though I were dressed up.'

'But you are dressed up.' She was wearing a fetching short dress, a very dark green in a shiny material, with a plunging neckline, and a diamond at the tip of the neck-vee.

'Well — I meant that a woman can use her surname like that when she wants to appeal to the kinkiness in men.'

'You mean it asserts a masculine prerogative.'

'Prerogative? Do you mean custom?'

'Yes, Ms Lindqvist.'

'I thought so.'

She paused, and then went on: 'But I did feel something about you that I must describe in my own language. I thought you had a spirit-guide. So I was not surprised to see you go into those transformations. Where I come from we call this trick — or custom —'

'Or prerogative —'

'Exactly — we call this prerogative the *Lindwurm*. People who can do it always have this spirit-guide. It is like something that doesn't belong, quite, but is with you, and is very powerful. Sometimes it is like a smell on the skin that doesn't belong to the personality; always it gives a little shiver. It is something that many women have, like a deeper mood, though it seems less incongruous or startling in them, since they are used to it.'

'Do you mean when they have their periods?'

'That's exactly what I do mean — but you couldn't be having a period, too, could you, Dr Pfoundes, unless you are *exceedingly* clever at transformations . . .' and she touched him with a sweet smile and a swift light caress across his trouser-fly.

* * *

'Do you know what witch's ointment is?'

'I have a feeling I'm going to find out.'

'Well, tell me what you think it is.'

'I've always assumed that it was a mixture of herbs people used to rub on their bodies to get a thrill.'

'What kind of thrill?'

'There were hallucinogens in it: monkshood, henbane and the like and they were absorbed through the skin.'

'Through the skin, Doctor? Is this how you apply drugs?'

'Well, I suppose there were bed-bug punctures and louse lesions and the like . . .'

'What a scabby lot the witches must have been.'

'Then there would have been something beastly in the ointment to make people feel important because they were doing evil. Like baby-fat.'

'What stuff you have been reading. That sounds like the monks talking.'

'Oh, you mean that it was particular skin? Mucus membrane that could absorb drugs?'

'Maybe. There used to be special dildoes made out of bulls' pizzles with ointment boxes attached.'

'Why did they include baby-fat?'

'A manner of speaking. It was menstrual blood, which you could say in a way was the body of a

59

baby.'

'Why menstrual blood?'

'Have you ever heard of pheromones, Doctor?' They had driven back to her place from the party. It was a large 'Stockbroker's Tudor' house not far from Wimbledon Common. She said it was her uncle's, who was away. They were in the big ground-floor lounge. He was relieved that there were no suits of armour, because there was oak panelling. She said she spent much of her time by herself in this house.

'What do you do?'

'I'm doing certain work that requires solitude. Usually, that is.'

'What do you do when you're not alone?'

'I'm about to find out, George.'

He was about to comment 'for the umpteenth time' then thought better of it. He found all this talk about witch-ointments rather seductive. He wondered what it would be like when she got down to it. No doubt she was wondering the same.

'I felt strange about my foot, it changing to my eyes like that. I'd call that a "positive hallucination" — when you see something that's not there.'

'You're sure it wasn't there?'

'Must you always talk in questions?'

'?'

'There is no doubt some potion I could have put on it to change it back again, like moly on Bottom's eye.' At this she gave a great guffaw. 'What's so funny?'

'It was love-in-idleness. Not moly. Moly was what Ulysses used to change his companions back from pigs after Circe had enchanted them.'

'They rose "goodlier than before" Homer says. It seems to have improved them.'

60

'Pigs have trotters too. I was just thinking of Bottom's eye. They say a woman has one more eye than a man.'

'How can that be? We've both got two nether eyes.'

'One of yours is on a stalk!' She reached out and touched him again. 'My eye is inside me. It is a cone that sits inside my vagina, and changes with the month, as the moon does, as the womb does.'

Pfoundes felt a very deep stirring in the roots of his penis. 'That is the cervix of the womb. A man never thinks of that.'

'They say that the women of the oracles of ancient times, the Pythia, would take the sacred snakes and allow them to lick their ears, so they could hear the oracle, their nostrils, so they could smell the oracle, their eyes, so that they could see the oracle, their mouths, so they could speak their oracle, their anuses, so they were clean for the oracle, and with its head deep inside, to lick the blood from the sacred oracle itself.'

'Then a prophetess would be having her period.'

'Certainly. It is then she throws off mortality, and is virgin.'

'I'm enjoying my sex-lecture, but could I have some more brandy, please?'

'I'll get it.'

As she got up, she paused, and he rose. He stepped towards her and she said 'My!' in a pleasant admiring fashion as she reached again and felt his penis through his trousers. 'Well, that's very, very good. There's not much need for more talk.' He found her zip and she stepped out of her dress, very white against the dark panelling. The air was sultry, and there was a distant rumble of thunder. He struggled out of his clothes. She walked over to the door and turned off the

61

light-switch — he felt surprised that she was the kind of woman who preferred the light out — then he realised he was mistaken as she went over to the big window-curtains and opened them by pulling at a cord. Outside he could see the darkly-glimmering lawn, set about with big bushes. There was a flash of lightning, and it looked like a stage on which hooded figures were waiting. She opened the french windows, and the fresh smell off the lawn swept in; he realised the rain was about to start.

'Would you like to try the witch-ointment?' She had a small, stoppered bottle in her hand. She pressed her smooth skin against him; it felt like the warm wings of moths.

'I hate drugs,' he said abruptly.

'No, my dear, this is a little sandalwood oil, that's all. I want to help you concentrate.'

That word reminded him of his skill in hypnosis; he had completely forgotten that he was that kind of person. He felt no desire to play hypnotic tricks, or to control the situation in any way. She came round behind him and he felt a small trickle of oil on the nape of his neck, and in the half-darkness her hand and the skin of his neck and upper shoulders seemed to get larger as she gently massaged him. She rubbed the oil over his shoulder-blades and down his spine, and his skin began to feel transparent, as if he were about to see her hands through it; if the lid would just quiver and rise, then his whole body would be an eye. What would he see then, what would this woman reveal herself as? She massaged his chest gently, paying particular attention to his breasts, which she emphasised with rolling clockwise caresses. His penis was straining forward, and felt more strongly rooted than he ever remembered, though

62

he was nowhere near ejaculation. In no sense was she masturbating him, only preparing him. She rubbed his diaphragm and he felt a warmness glow there, and he knew this was a true hypnosis, with no compulsion or direction in it, only discovery. His penis felt like the high pommel of a saddle that was his lower body and which carried him. His buttocks were the sturdy conches of this saddle, and there was a hollowness behind which seemed to reach right forward from his anus into the tip of his penis. Then there was a sudden click of awareness and he understood that the feeling was more as though he were riding an animal with a pointed head, he was astride this hollow charger or hobby-horse of an organ, like a broomstick that was alive. Then he was a centaur and not the rider of this horse, he was not separate from it at all, it was not 'his', it was him. The woman was massaging the underbelly of this centaur with light and sound that flickered round the room and brought him back to his human form for a moment. He looked down his penis, which still gave him the feeling of something he bestrode that was hollow behind and one organ from anus to urethra: she had been massaging him underneath in the perineum between anus and scrotum, and he felt very alive there, but there was a hollowness, as if his anus had pleasantly split and extended forward to make a vagina just at the root of his thrust, the tip of which felt ready to burst. He looked down at it and saw a dark patch there, as though it were bleeding — he touched it and tried to see what had got on it by lifting his finger nearer his eye: 'Don't worry,' she said, 'it's my blood.'

'Come into the garden,' she whispered, and she led him over the threshold of the windows. The grass

63

was very cool to his feet; as he stepped on it he suddenly saw a flash of crushed grass-blades, as though he could see through the soles of his feet. The breeze caressed his skin, or was it her breath as her mouth moved over his body? He found that her lips were touching his feet and he heard her whisper 'Blessed be . . . Blessed be thy feet that brought thee here . . .' and he felt her touch on lips, throat, navel, and then her lips were round his penis inviting him to thrust.

Then they were at his lips again, tasting salt. A whisper, 'The rain will break all the clouds,' and suddenly he saw a drop of water land on his skin, like her touch, but a little scintilla, a flash of light. That was before the garden lit up in the next lightning-flash, he was sure, but then he was not so sure because the garden stayed as bright as lightning as the rain fell and light came flooding into his skin from it. He found that she had turned round and he was deep inside her from behind and they were riding together towards an impossible consummation which loomed taller and taller through the streams of light. Her face was turned round over her shoulder watching him and as they rode together it seemed to change, but he couldn't be sure, so bright was the light from his skin and all his body as the rain fell, and he was only a direction made of light galloping towards the great mountain deep within her the tip of which was missing in the sky, and whose canter led to other worlds that were opening to him. Many people rose with him through that sky, and as he rode he was sometimes hare and sometimes hound, and once a stallion and an elephant and his mother and his father riding, and like a pack of cards his body and hers spread through the firmament and on all the cards were pictures of people riding. And her face looked back over its shoulder and was snake and sleepy turtle and guru and baby and long-dead corpse and he was struggling in a delta of marsh and then she was a horse and he was riding and they were circling round and round the bald mountain looking down deep into the crater which was banded with all the strata right into the centre of the earth. And then the mountain lifted its head and unfurled its wings and nodded five times rather slowly and looked straight into his eyes and at that moment, he saw, nature *smiled* and he knew that he would always ride in that smile wherever he was or whatever he was doing. Which he now recollected, on a suburban lawn, his penis deep inside a perfect stranger, but now shrinking away from one of the most satisfactory experiences he had ever had, unravelling itself back to ordinary life, retreating from its burrow, relaxation pouring through his being, the woman looking over her shoulder and smiling at him, and in the last peal of thunder, an echo of that eternal *smile* with its acknowledgment that would never leave his deep core banded with all its strata.

The rain was only pattering now, and it merely felt cold, a little, and glittered as it fell. He gave a great sigh, she turned and kissed him. 'You are smiling. Did you see my Devil?' she asked. He nodded, smiling, and deeply happy. 'Well, well, that was a bit of a silly symphony, a bit operatic. I wonder which language you saw in: yours or mine? Or something in between, that we can improve on as the days go by.'

Pfoundes led the way indoors. She took up the brandy decanter and the glasses, and led the way upstairs to a warm bedroom. He asked for the bathroom, and she showed him where it was, on the other side of the bedroom. There was a slightly-sunken

green bath with a shower. 'Shall we . . .?' he said,
pointing to the bath. 'No, never now,' she replied,
frowning a little. 'You must not wash it off.' She
opened a linen cupboard and took out two white
towelling robes, ironed and dry. 'Put this on for a
minute and have your brandy. Then we must go to
bed. It will be the first time I have slept with a man
for nearly two years. I was advised to wait.' Later,
skin glowing under the duvet, but ordinarily —
ideally, like a moment of perfect health — she whispered in his ear: 'Thank you, Satan, thank you.'

* * *

'I could make the blind see,' said Pfoundes, 'if I could
help them to concentrate. I think of the splendour of
the robes of the patriarchs. They are surely clothing
themselves artificially in what is given to them
naturally; only they don't want too much of it, not
a thunder-rain of it, with their gold crowns. The most
successful music-hall comedian ever known dressed
as a clergyman, and he carried an umbrella. That was
enough to make them laugh, and keep on laughing.
The curate whose profession is to keep God's rain
from wetting his head. The music-hall audiences
oppressed by church and state laughed as a sign of
their understanding, shared and depicted by the
slapstick comedian.
    'If I can remember what happened, then I could
build a machine,' says Pfoundes. 'In this am I not
like the patriarchs and bishops, with their brocaded
capes and vests telling the tales of the mythology
they have chosen, seen once and fixed for ever,
covering up the undeveloped photographs of the
skin? Well, not for myself perhaps — which is the

66

way they must have reasoned, with their vicarious succession. But if I'm to make the blind see, it would be better to set up in practice with a machine, rather than to welcome all to sexual rites and sacred shower-baths, taurobolia of blood in which a bull is disembowelled above the trench in which an initiate stands, or crouches with his lady rider or steed, having sex, to see the pictures over the skin, with the hot bull blood full of cries and proto-spunk like stars to stand in for his thunderstorm. The soiled garments are stripped off, like the hide of a snake easing off the new glossy body, that sees, covered with eyes!

'That was the central experience: I saw with my whole hide of touch. I saw our journey to orgasm (and conception, as it happened, a child made in the rain of blood, a moon-child made at the period) by body-light. I saw her womb with its Fallopian wings, and I saw the vessel of life smiling, as it gathered the dead things and gave them life. I think I saw with my nose too, as a dog does; those riders on the wind, why, some of them were the great coiling perfume-pictures pulled out of the lawn and the lawn's laurels. I saw the hoofbeats of my own blood, and hers too, and the galloping, swimming snakes of our bodies, and the greater body of which we were an executant part, the thunderstorm. It was as if I were a thin layer of eyes living in the skin, some looking inwards and some looking outwards, all the eyes opening simultaneously in our orgasm, seeing by lightning and body-light. A blind man could see by body-light.

'Did I hear the lightning or see the thunder? Nature does not divide. We blind the eyes by giving them spectacles. The blind man lives in a dark room in which he may see visions, his eyes turned inwards. This is for the blind who are rich, maybe; blindness multiplies greatly the blinding difficulties of making a living.

'So if I made a machine to pick up the impulses generated by one organ responding to life, and feed it back to another organ, then I would unite the senses. The psychedelic drugs do it: you can taste size, see time. The grandfather clock is a good hypnotist; standing on the stair he sounds as the mounting path to sleep looks. Therefore I must have rhythm and time, and I must be able to change time about, so that a man may relive his life in a few moments, perhaps relive it anew, from the time he was a child, and could see everything.

'They call skin a "hide" because we cloak ourselves in what we have blinded. I want my subjects to concentrate on what is actually happening to them, I want them to recollect, to collect themselves again. And myself. I want to dream awake, and dream as I am touched, and as I touch. It will be called the Pfoundes Oscilloscope, because it will cause the senses to oscillate the one to the other until a new sense is formed.

'I will start with the lie-detector, since I am concerned to detect that lie of blindness that all men and some women indulge in. I shall construct a Super-Polygraph. If an instrument is constructed so as to monitor the blood-pressure by a band around the arm, the heart-rate by a stethoscope on the chest, with a band about the chest too for the rate of breathing, electrodes on the skin to detect its sweating and conductivity, and a needle in the finger for the blood-flow, and one feeds this to a spool of paper through a comb of recording needles, why, there is the Polygraph. "Did you, on the night of September 2, 1947, fuck this lady in a thunderstorm and become risible?" "Certainly not, Officer, I never did." But the Polygraph has a fit, because I breathe heavily, remembering her, I sweat, remembering her; my blood-pressure rises to fill my cock, remembering her; and my blood certainly flows, since I am alive remembering her. The officer knows, because my body speaks the truth. And the truth is more fascinating than the lie. So if I show a blind man the truth, he will see. "Truth can never be told so as to be understood, and not be believ'd."

'Now then, I must connect the skin to the eyes, the eyes to the nose, the nose to the ears, and the tongue to the skin. I must amplify the visual input and change it into electric patterns, as the actors in the television studios, and the Queen at Glamis, and the whole of Scotland, and the Atlantic Ocean, are changed into radio waves which are turned into electric patterns in the television set. But I will let them run as patterns of heat over the skin, I shall have the patient sit in a chair which is a gigantic television tube, but a blind one, that makes its patterns of heat and cold. The cameras will be trained on his body, and the sight of himself will be changed to the skin-feeling of himself, and he will see himself through his skin.

'Then I will have a seeing television tube, in colour, and whatever is said to him or he says, passing through his ears, will be changed into coloured patterns or images, and I will have a computer that selects simple pictures for the words I use. I will have a sonar scan in the room, that will take a picture by super-sonic vibrations of the innermost conjunctions and massages of his organs the one with the other, and when he speaks, the shape of the air-cavities he is forming will affect the pictures on the screen, and the scents that will be caused to permeate the room by a system of fans blowing air over stoppering and unstoppering bottles. I will feed the skin-resistance to the eyes and the respiration to the ears: he shall hear the great lolloping of approaching sleep. I shall cross sight with scent, doublecross sound with touch, and countercross taste with time, by offering him a mouth-organ which plays him: a little chest of complex tastes that you put between your teeth and it squirts harmoniously over your taste-buds, or rinses them with a little pure spring water. I shall pick up his brain-waves from his scalp and play them back over his skin, and I shall pick up his skin-waves and pump them back into his brain. He will live in a world in which his every movement is the crumbling of an ant-hill or a swarm of stars. Into this world I shall say, "Look at this great lion, it is bold, it fears nothing." And by this word I shall create in his world a great lion that fears nothing, and the lion will be made out of himself, and will be him. I shall say, "Ride this lion, and scatter your enemies"; he will do so. I shall say, "Take up your bed and walk." And I shall bring the dead back to life by saying into this world (supposing I had died) "George Frederick Pfoundes lives, and lives, and lives"; and my patient will talk to me, care for me, pay my bills and make love to me as if I were really there; and perhaps I shall be made again by these means, should I die.

'But what if my teaching dies with me? That would be too bad. Then I must make haste to construct my machine.'

As we have seen, it was not nearly so grand as his first thoughts intended. This was merely because the feedback was so strong on the audio-visual channels only that people dropped immediately into the

70

deepest trance of which they were capable. It was like the commercial channels on TV, supposing that the market-research link had been much abbreviated. As if the camera had got into your home, and when the set said 'Eat Booby-bars' watched what you did. If you made yourself some toast, the set would then modify its advertisement so that it said 'Eat Toasted Booby-Bars.' If you put honey on the toast, then 'Eat Toasted Booby-Bars with Honey.' Or as if the insurance companies ran the medical centres: the more people that died, the more they had to pay up, so it was much better to spend money on preventive medicine, and have capital assets; and they might as well endow teaching departments at the universities too. It was simply feed-back, it was simply seeing what was possible and bringing it about in the interests of the most powerful minds: it was simply society. Society is a Pfoundes Oscilloscope, gone wrong. And when the Pfoundes Polygraphic Oscilloscope went wrong, that was only because it was too powerful by half, or the things it uncovered in people were.

'What does my skin look like by loudspeaker,' Pfoundes asked himself, 'or my cerebral cortex by television? I shall call it "creating a Sphinx" or "creating the *Lindwurm*" since I will have the eyes of a hawk or a lynx, the nose of a dog or a jackal, the hearing of a gazelle, the touch of a dolphin, that extends through the ocean. Why, I must be a poet — what is a good analyst but a man who responds to images, or a hypnotist but a man who creates them in others? Perhaps a doctor is a poet who actually *does* something, a priest who causes the god to appear in truth. This is the god of healing, and the polygraph is ill-called the lie-detector, since it detects the truth. It is the lie which awakes the animal to take revenge,

71

the truth which conceives.'

How could Pfoundes be thought a madman? It might be nonsense, but it was true nonsense. His lovebook sold two million, and is still selling. After the blind man died from seeing too much, Pfoundes turned his Oscilloscope off, until his last and greatest experiment that concerned the God of Death.

* * *

'The eagle is in bitter anguish.' The blotting-pad was covered with fragments of writing, cloudy scraps. 'Give me your handbag-mirror, Persy,' I said to my pregnant witch, 'I want to read your obstetrician's secrets from his blotting-pad. Hope his instruments are cleaner.' She gave me a sharp look. 'I suppose witches' accoucheurs are supposed to use fingers only, and not haggle about their fees.'

'Please don't tease, Fred. We ought to take everything quite seriously. You know what we think about her trance.'

'Oh well, you're in a trance, and the baby inside you too, so everything we say or do is a suggestion that may make the baby grow, or hinder her. I'm not sure it is her.'

'The pendulum . . .'

'Oh, I haven't time for sexing by the pendulum. Your body knows it, and we'll see whether your mind interprets your body aright.'

'I feel death . . .'

'Persy, I can't have you talking like that.'

'But death is a happy thing . . .' She started weeping quietly.

'If you're unhappy, Persy, use your trance. One . . . two . . . three . . .'

'No, I'm *so* happy. Really. I don't want to go.'

'You're not going anywhere. You're going to have your baby and bring it up like an ordinary child.'

'An ordinary witch-child.'

'All right then. An ordinary witch-hypnotist child.'

'Let's call her Hypnotich.'

I was glad to see her laugh after the awful dream last night when she saw her ancestors come through the wall for her, and before going back into the wall with them she had fed the baby and changed its nappy and handed the child to me. She said that in her dream she knew that when she walked backwards into the stone and merged with it, she left a faintly-smiling death-mask on the wallpaper. 'It was here,' she said, stroking the breakfast-room wall. I gave her hypnosis to calm her, and then it was time to go to see the obstetrician.

The blotting-case was black plastic, with thin gold trapeze-lines embossed. It opened in two hinged flaps on to the sullied paper I was reading with Persy's mirror to kill the time. Trier should have got his nurse to change the paper: it gave an impression of imprecision and unfinished business. There was a printed card stuck into one of the pockets. It read 'Dogerty Funeral Parlour: Discretion, Sympathy, Economy. G. Macnamara: qualified Funeral Director.' I would speak to Trier. He should certainly look to what was left around in his waiting-room: here was a patient advertising for a client, who would be an unsuccessful ex-patient. A doctor should not be supposed to have failures! One would go in to him with the suggestion of death, advertised in the outer room. I looked for the card to show him: I must have put it in a pocket. I rummaged. No matter.

A suggestion of death, like Persy's dream. A foul suggestion, like a pregnant woman with bad breath. Persy's breath had always been sweet until she had started vomiting with morning sickness. I could not speak to her about this. Why ever should I? Dreams of death were beneficial: they indicated change. But in a pregnant woman. She should dream of architecture, of giving birth.

I tilted the mirror over a promising passage in violet ink. I read: 'Is it Racine?' and then a partial sentence containing the words *'L'anguille . . . angoisse'*. *Angoisse* was 'anguish' all right, but *anguille* was 'eel' or certain kinds of lug-worm, in French, not 'eagle'. 'The eagle is in bitter anguish' was my idea of Racine, never having read him. Perhaps the eagle had worms.

'Doctor will see you now.' Trier's appalling spotty-chinned nurse came out of his inner sanctum. He was an excellent doctor, but did not understand the curative powers of pretty females in the practice, amounting to a hypnotic influence. I had always made my nurses wear vivid make-up under the strip-lighting, so that they looked twice as alive as the patients. 'This is how you *should* look,' was the suggestion. I followed Persy into Trier's surgery, and I pulled the marked blotting-pad from its clean underneath first, and pocketed it.

'Good morning, Ms Lindqvist. Hello, Pfoundes. Let's see how the baby's getting on.' Persy lay down on the leatherette couch that was covered with a clean paper sheet. I hate using paper sheets: like something out of a funeral parlour. Persy lay with her tummy towering like Silbury Hill. Trier's hands looked large and particularly strong against her white belly. 'Ah, ah, beautiful,' he intoned, and I could tell he was speaking the truth. 'LOA. Fine presentation —' darting a glance at me '— nothing could be better.' Then he showed Persy where the baby's head was by pinching the belly very firmly below it. 'Perfect, perfect. Let's listen now.' He carefully slid the disc of his stethoscope around the tummy, then slipped the earpieces off and gave them to Persy. She was surprised, but put them in her ears — and then a slow smile spread across her face, and stayed there. 'May I listen?' I said, after a while. She didn't hear me. I caught her eye, and smiled. She took the ear-pipes off and gave them to me. I fitted the springy apparatus into my ears.

It was a sound I had heard many times before, but never from my own. At first I heard nothing, but that was because I had been hearing it from the instant I put the plastic earpieces in, and it was so great and so soft a sound that one's ordinary everyday ears had to tune themselves to it. It was like the soft galloping of horses. It was a misty sound, with a certain edge of decision to it. It was definite, yet so fast that its outlines blurred. Yet it was like the galloping of horses, near and far away at the same moment, as though I were both the rider and somebody listening to the horse coming towards me, over soft cinders, deep turf. It is the deepest sound that I have ever heard, this foetal heartbeat that was galloping towards me. Who was it bringing, what rider through the mists of the other world? *L'anguille angoisse* ... Soon it would burst out of that world, like somebody exiled and escaping over the border. I wished god-speed into that babe through the tubes of that stethoscope deep into its mother, those hoofbeats galloping out of the twin tunnels. This deep sound from the other world ... the deepest sound ... so

75

deep ... the very voice of the trance of life before birth ... I must certainly incorporate it into hypnotic procedure. I handed the stethoscope back to Trier, smiled at him, and rubbed my hands briskly.

PART TWO

A Posthumous Suggestion

With incomparable briskness my father walked into the room. 'Hoopsa! Hoopsa! Boyso!' that was the strange cry he brought with him, only silently, into my head. He moved with such vigour, such decision, he shone! I suppose he must have dandled me as a baby and called to the little child as to dogs 'Hoopsa! Hoopsa! Boyso!' and like a dog I always came running to him: it was as though his energy created whirlpools one could only watch with big shining eyes like hanging mirrors, or if one came nearer one would go round and round and plunge to the centre, offer a hug or a kiss, which he would pause to receive before bustling on, on to the next job, his buttons shining on his dark suit, his hair sleekly brilliantined back, his high forehead stream-lined by these shining wings. 'Angela!' he would say in a surprised way, but with a smile. 'Why, Angela, my angel, how nice,' and then he would be through the room and out of the door as if walking a ward in a bustle of students. I hated him for it, and loved him too. I could not be who I was when he was there, but since he seemed altogether a more vital and interesting thing than I was, I wanted to learn to be like him.

I suppose he had always been hypnotising me, but when does soothing your child lovingly with caresses and private words merge into hypnosis? I think I know, and it had nothing to do with his wishing to exercise a Svengali control on his only daughter. It is that I *remember* a deliberate hypnotic session: I suppose I must have been eight. Long before this, though, I know there had been vivid dreams that may have come from him, since on my own I seldom dreamed. There were memories, too, that cannot have been actual: I remember a nest of black and white rabbits in my bedroom once — yes, a nest of them, all cuddled together in twigs. 'Look at the nest of rabbits, Angela,' and I saw them, 'look how cuddly they are, and how sleepy,' and then I was asleep, though I remembered enough to look for them in the morning. They were not there. I recall another time when I was frightened of a thunderstorm, and my father spoke comforting words to me, and I saw kind faces in the clouds uttering the loud words, and when the lightning came it came slowly, or so I saw it, and it was like a jagged slice into a sweet fruit whose juice was light which I could taste. Later, I heard of the magical use of fires, that 'opened the doors of distance'. This is another way of putting what happened to me then.

The deliberate hypnotic session was in my father's consulting-room. It was long before the Feedback Oscilloscope had become established and famous; indeed, after I got my degree I helped my father develop the instrument, so some of the credit (if that is what one should call it) was mine. The big door was open, and I had strayed along the corridor leading to it, which I had been told not to do. I peeped round the door; there he was at his desk, and he was in a reverie. The desk-light made the big reclining-chair opposite him shine. He looked up and saw me quite soon — I think it was the first time I had seen him still for any length of time. He sprang up. 'Come, Angela — I'll teach you real magic!' and he took me by the hand and made me lie down on the couch. At once my eyelids would not stay open, and a warm comforting flow went through me, as though I was afloat in a deep brown river, and I was not sure where my body ended and the river began. 'Don't go to sleep, my girl. You'll not learn anything if you sleep. You are simply very very relaxed.' And I was. 'Very very aware' and I was, aware it seemed like an aerial photograph might be aware of itself, a remote pattern, but every detail sharply focussed. 'Think of your fingernail, your little fingernail on your right hand,' he said, and I saw it, pink, the cuticle pressed back from the half-moon, as my nanny had taught me, with orange-sticks. 'It's moving, Angie, moving by itself,' and now I felt it wiggling slowly to and fro, and I could see it doing that too, behind my closed lids. 'Now your whole hand is very very light, as though there were a hydrogen balloon tied to it, and very very slowly, without your doing anything, lifting it from the chair,' and I felt my hand shift a little, like a dirigible in its moorings, and slowly rise as though that airship had been let carefully free, nudging from its moorings, and my hand moved of itself like a light air-filled bladder or a soap-bubble and it was so pleasing a sensation that I laughed out loud because there was a deep tension of laughter in the pit of my lungs which was part pleasure and part amazed irritation. 'Higher, higher, Angie,' and up it went, I laughing out loud with undiluted pleasure now at my father's extreme cleverness at being able to get inside my body and pull the strings, like a puppet-master or a baby able to make its mother

81

do whatever it wanted.

'Now, whenever you count five and click your fingers you will be in this deep trance of relaxation, and then, whatever you tell yourself to do, you will be able to do, whatever you wish for and see clearly enough in your mind's eye will come to pass, even things you could not believe were possible.' Oh then, a terrible thing happened, because I saw a clear picture of my father struck down by the gleaming bumpers of a car, and I looked through the windscreen and saw my own face driving it. But that picture passed, and in later time I learnt to change the pictures if they got out of command, as they sometimes did.

My nanny once took me to where my mother had been burned, and showed me a little memorial tablet on which was written her name and the date of her birth, and that of her death, which was my birthday. She showed me this, and then took me inside to the little chapel, and told me I must say my prayers. I did not like the chapel, and though I had learnt the Lord's Prayer and how to say 'God Bless Daddy and Nanny and my Dear Mummy who lives in the land we shall all come to' I would not say that now. Into my head had sprung my mother's lean face from the photograph, and I wished her to stay dead. The prayer had come to pass before I had been born. I did not understand my wish, or like it. What I did understand when my father hypnotised me was that the state he called trance was like this same thing that other people called prayer, and in which dangerous things happened, even to God. Before I gave up prayer, I had killed and humiliated God many times, and thought myself eternally damned for doing so. It was easier to keep my mind on my own desires, with the help of my father's hypnotism-magic.

* * *

There had been singing most of the night. When it woke her in the small hours she thought it was a gramophone. Some party with the volume turned up in the house by the docks. Then the regular beat of the singing broke into irregular squeals and bass shouts. So it was not a gramophone.

She watched dawn slide into the right-hand side of her hotel window, with the singing still echoing from somewhere among the houses that skirted the hill. The sun's rising charged the air with mists that muffled the music, so that instead of sound, light now held her wakeful attention. There grew first a grey tinny light full of the dissolved ice of the night's darkness, then there was a red blush in the sky like the dull red of heated iron. A breath of wind took all the sound into itself. A black coil of birds flourished suddenly into the air, descended again. She realised she had been listening to birdsong for some time, but without being aware of it. The false dawn died away, and a cool misty light made the sea dark green-grey. Now the disc of the sun of May Day rose too dazzling to look at, staring in at the window-pane.

It was far too early for hotel breakfast or early morning tea. She left the window and sat down in an armchair with a science-fiction paperback she had bought in London. She loved SF: in her father's words it was full of *suggestions,* vivid, convincing suggestions that were gradually becoming reality.

The reality of this tale was not a cheering one. It was the story of a woman's quest through a world of

83

earth's future. The whole surface of the planet was covered with skyscrapers a thousand floors high. Rich people lived in the sunlit penthouses and roof-gardens of the topmost storey: the chairmen and executives of the vast corporations that owned the world. The less rich occupied successive layers downward, and their windows were illumined by sun for fewer and fewer hours of the day as the apartments descended in price. Society was strictly stratified. Storeys numbered as low as two hundred were crammed with the poor, the uncontrollable, the criminal, the violent.

The heroine of this tale wandered from the rich sunlit layers of her birth, down through many social strata, in which she found the manners and disorders of former times fossilised by custom. She served apprenticeships to many modes of life: as courtesan, doctor, hydroponics attendant, policewoman; she broke down and was institutionalised on the third layer as an accredited lunatic (who could never see the light of the moon) and after she was discharged as cured she became a beggar.

Now she had found her way down to the lowest gulf of the buildings, as a rag-picker on the disused asphalts of the roadways. The air down there was a different substance from the sunny air of her birth: it was full of all the heavy gaseous waste of all the people who lived, and though the hydroponics inlets sucked much of the carbon dioxide off the streets to feed the plants in the great artificially-lit cities, there were still rumours of invisible tidal-waves of the unbreathable gas, that rolled many storeys high through the streets and struck underprivileged people down in their hundreds.

This air, which was just breathable, was thick and

clouded with big flakes of dust that fell continually from the high buildings. She had bought out of her meagre savings the big yellow plastic protective helmet that was intended to protect her from the more dangerous and sudden detritus that also fell from the buildings — beer-cans, crockery, spent bullets, an occasional human corpse — but it was her task to gather into her bag the big fluffy accumulations of fibre that were wound of this dust as it twisted restlessly in the city breezes. These swatches, very light entanglements of fibre chafed from people's clothes, mixed with sandy dust from the buildings' sills and flakes from human skin worn in the endless rubbing and jostling of the city's affairs, could be reprocessed into paper and cheap simulated cloth. She had also had to buy the rake with which she stalked a big dust-ball that had rolled itself into the size of a bus, turned over and over in the constant stale street-breezes. It would cram down in her bag to a piece of entanglement the size of a cricket ball, but that was something to be going on with. As she turned a towering grey corner she saw a gang of her rival pickers closing in on her dust-ball, armed also with rakes, and pitchforks as well. She clutched her rake, knowing in advance that she had lost the fight, and that she would probably be stabbed and stripped of her remaining rags and left in the litter of these endless streets to gradually dry out into the stone like a stain, and be blown gently to pieces by the gritty breezes.

Angela came abruptly out of her story before that happened. The human singing was louder now, and larger, than any birdsong. It had entered the early morning streets. She could hear the words:

Unite and unite and let us all unite,
For summer is a-come unto day,
And whither we are going we will all unite,
In the merry morning of May.

'I'm sure we shall,' thought Angela, with her head cocked to the music, 'but where that might be I'm not sure.' She got up and looked out of the window. The streets were still shaded, and there were flashes of white, furtive as white shadows, as the inhabitants of the town dressed for the part began to gather for the dance. She looked further out; the water of the bay was quite still, as if listening to the music and the song with its tall, conched sand-dunes on the opposite shore. She thought she could hear echoes thrown back by these dunes. Tucked in among them were the grey fragments of a ruined church, half-hidden.

Breakfast in the hotel dining-room cheered her. The sun was strong and hot as she sat at her solitary table, and it threw panels of yellow light across the dark carpet; yellow and appetising as the scrambled egg heaped on squares of toast the young waitress put before her. All the waitresses this morning wore their black and white uniforms as if this were an ordinary day, but they each had a bunch of bright flowers tucked in at their waist or tied to their belt. Her fellow-breakfasters were all smiling and talking, and she felt the lack of a companion. She wished, and did not wish, that her father were there: he would be spruce and bright enough for the morning, as intelligent and alert as she hoped to be on this visit to one of the few Pagan ceremonies of May Day left in Britain, at Padstow in Cornwall — the famed day of the 'Obby 'Oss. This image of the prancing beast that conjured Maytime fertility out of the land and the people, like a great hypnotist, was a worthy study indeed. It was not a Victorian folk-fake or revival; not at all. This dance had gone on in this village each year for unbroken centuries, for as long as there had been written or carved or painted records. Pfoundes wanted this power for himself, or, rather, incorporated into science for the sake of humanity. Angela was a scout sent; next year they would film and take recordings. It was said that the locals did not like records taken, but they would meet that problem when they came to it. Sellers of the printed broadsheet of the 'Obby 'Oss song, it was said, had been elbowed into the harbour, since the song should be learnt and not peddled and haggled over — or that was the custom. Pfoundes of course would meet energy with energy, even if the result were violence. He referred to the 'Oss as a 'witch-cult'. If this were so, then it was surprising that it had lasted so long.

Back in her bedroom, Angela tidies up before going out, and hunts in a drawer for handkerchiefs. She looks out at the high tide between the corridor of town and scalloped dunes. It is her high tide, which is why she was restless last night. Even now this period probably wouldn't come; they were scanty and irregular, an irritating intermittent malaise accompanied by fretful and ill-understood dreams that did not respond to hypnotic techniques.

Movement in the street below catches her eye. There is a flash of light in a great dark disc that is moving jerkily. It is the 'Oss, surrounded by his white-clad acolytes dancing, and he prances turning and swaying. He is like an enormous shiny black wheel of patent leather, with a tall pointed hat, and great white mustachios and staring eyes that make a confusing pattern. There he goes, spinning and dipping with a red mouth through the brightening streets to the sound of an accordion and a drum.

Arise up missus and gold be your ring
For summer is a-come unto day
And give to us a cup of ale the merrier we shall sing,
In the merry morning of May.

It is a man dressed in a great wheel covered with tarpaulin. His body penetrates the wheel, which is held on his shoulders by straps like braces. He wears on his head the steepled black hat and on the front of his face the confusing mask. You can see his white legs dancing under the long black shiny skirt. There are red ribbons at the tip of the tall hat. At the rim of the disc is a little wooden horse's head, whose jaws clatter as they snap: the man inside pulls a string that does that as he dances. The wooden disc is heavy, and swings from side to side. Angela sees that the figures who accompany it, the little band and the dancers with flowers in their belts and red sashes, are all children. This is the Children's 'Oss, then, and it must be a boy dancing inside the mask.

But dancing in front of the 'Oss is an intent little red-headed girl. She holds a velvet embroidered heart-shape fastened to a stick, like a big, padded, sequined lollipop. She waves it in front of the 'Oss's nose as she dances, and he is teased to run forward, or stop in his tracks, or recoil, as though he were playfully pretending to devour the heart which the little girl holds out to him in her dance. She has the expression — intent, firm and sensitive — of a lady judo-player, utterly serious and absorbed. Angela knows that she is called the Teazer. Evidently, however, the 'Oss has his wishes also, because he pauses in his dance, leaving his Teazer standing in mid-step, and grasps the knocker of a front door with his 'snapper', giving a hard knock. The door immediately opens, and the children troop in, the 'Oss standing aside. Then he tilts his shiny black skirts, since he is too big for the door, and pulls his head out of the disc and the head-mask. It is a man underneath, not a boy: he is almost a dwarf, and his face is shiny with sweat. He leans the 'Oss-body against the front of the house and follows the children through the front door. There will be something for his thirst in there. The street is empty as if it had never been full, and the white children led by their extraordinary companion seem apparitions of a fairy-tale: the white-clad, capering children with their red ribbons; the contented little band banging away; and who could have made up such a thing as that 'Oss, all of black and full of reflections from its shiny coat, a great open mouth gaping on its head with painted in that mouth a grinning fringe of pointed white teeth, and an immense tongue lolling out and dangling down like a bib? Yet it was their familiar, whom they knew. Angela could still hear singing in the empty street.

The bright sea flashes the light between the twining waves of the dunes and the dressed and upright hollow stones of the town, and the fused particles that flash in the granite and the loose particles of the sand play with the song as with the light, dividing it into flashes and echoes from every grain, and uniting it into pulses off the sea which break up again as the wind that carries the sound beats on the water and up the streets. 'That is uniting!' says Angela as she watches the lights in the water and listens to the song from the streets. The brave figure of the little red-haired Teazer with her monstrous consort pleases her, and the expression on her face and the attitude of her body: the deliberate placing of the hips so that the balance changed but was never lost, a flowing and winning thing. It was (and this was how the image of the judo exponent came to her) like a fight that was a game, that one must join to keep one's end up, certainly, but not to overcome. The expression of the girl was dauntless; yes, that was it, the partner of the 'Oss was a Dauntless Girl, and she learnt her courage in partnership with whatever forces the wheeling, dipping, flashing, jet-black personage represented. Certainly once the mask went on, the dancer became something more than a man, something much larger and sure of itself, as though a wave of the sea had rolled the essence of the moonless night in itself, and had put on a pointed hat, and, clutching a little wooden spar of a horse, had come riding tall as houses into the harbour, wearing a complicated face of foaming eyebrows and deep watery mouths, and flashing the sunshine into many lights within itself. As it was the high tide of the new moon, that meant that sun and moon were united, pulling the waters in their tidal wave together in a straight line, the sight of the moon lost within the sun's disc, but its power and gravity felt in every particle of the sea, and in all water. Moon and sun are risen together on this May Day, she realised.

She had only seen the Children's 'Oss so far, and that had made a difference to her, though she was not sure yet what difference. It was something to do with her father. It was as though the 'Oss, with his complicated colours and startling appearance, looked mad, but was not mad. Instead, it was deeply natural. Its dance both moved and stayed in the same place, and all the people were united by it. Her father, though, looked sane and behaved reasonably, but what he did was mad, utterly mad. He was like golden butter melting on a hot plate, dashing around shining; or like a piece of metallic sodium thrown on to water: that too would dash around and burst into yellow flame. Yet he was like a natural force.

But was it not madness to prefer a painted mask to one's father? A two-faced mask at that. Those bushy white eyebrows of the 'Oss: they were the key to the complication of the face, which was in fact two faces at once. The sight of him buzzed, as it were, because one's interpretation oscillated rapidly between the two. If you read the 'eyebrows' as the *moustaches* of the creature, then the red patches above were meat-dish-sized eyes, glaring like the traditional bug-eyed monster of SF. If you read those hairy ridges, those eyebrows as *eyebrows,* however, then the creature had no eyes at all beneath its bushy brows, just a black expanse divided by the sharp streaks of red and white that represented a long nose, above the gaping mouth and hanging tongue like a red flannel bib. Or else it was dancing serenely with its black eyelids closed. Then you looked again and saw it watching you out of those red pits. Its face was both open and closed, awake and asleep, alive and dead: it hovered between the two states, like hypnosis itself. It was a Blind Seer, a Blind Black Dancer who could see where he was dancing.

A brightly-dressed crowd of people flows past the end of the empty street which stretches away below her window. She comes out of her reverie and remembers that she must leave the protecting hotel with its safe windows and, with all the other people, meet the grown-up horse in the springtime streets. She knows that this version of the 'Oss is larger — the disc or hoop which supports the shiny tarpaulin of the skirt will be a full seven feet across. She had heard too that *this* 'Oss — as befits any grown-up drama — *dies,* and it is this death which brings his companions in the dance and their spectators into more abundant life, and it is done again and again as part of the jollity.

There is a tradition that it will never rain in the town on May Day. Angela is out in the sunlight now. A great wealthy yacht has come into the harbour. The spanking white ship with honey-coloured decking is thickly decorated with green boughs. There is a table set for drinking on the poop deck, and cardboard boxes of wine under it. There is a car parked in the harbour yard, its windows all steamed up from the sleepers within: they were not going to pay a hotel for the privilege of watching what should be free to all. But they would miss what they came for unless they rose soon.

> *Arise up missus and gold be your ring*
> *For summer is a-come unto day*

The fishing-boats in the harbour are garlanded like maypoles, and they rock in the gentle swell with a random and sleepy clanking of the loose metal in their rigging. Angela turns the corner, following the music, into the press of people, and soon she is thickly packed into the press. As she is tall she can on tiptoe see a swirling black as of a cloak beyond the people, which dips and wheels, and she can see the top hat of the Presenter: the man who precedes the procession of 'Obby 'Oss and Teazer, dancers and band.

92

The young women of Padstow might if they would,
For summer is a-come unto day,
They might have made a garland with the white rose
*   and the red*
In the merry morning of May.

The crowd sways to the music, not in a systematic way, but in an organic way, like a big bush thickly set with head-berries. The leaves are a-tremble, she thinks, every leaf on the human tree.

Unite and unite and let us all unite,
For summer is a-come unto day,
And whither we are going we will all unite,
In the merry morning of May

The slight movements and nudgings of the people allow her to slip her way into the clearing in which the 'Oss dances with his people, and she abruptly comes free into this, and sees a sight she was not prepared for: the great 'Oss sinking to his knees.

The tenor of the song has changed too, and it is now a mournful dirge:

O! where is St George,
* O, where is he O?*
He is out on his long-boat all on the salt sea O.
Up flies the kite and down falls the lark O.
Aunt Ursula Birdhood she had an old Ewe
And she died in her own Park O

The Teazer — a scarlet-flushed man with a red sash and the bright garland wilting in his belt — is pointing his lollipop-sceptre with the satin heart on it towards the ground, and the 'Oss settles slowly down, his skirt billowing around the disc, the steeple-crowned head bowing. The dancers are still, their

93

faces serious and intent. The Teazer is motionless, pointing his sceptre. The song dies away and there is a silence. No one moves. Then — with a sudden rush, quite unprepared for, the 'Oss springs up — no longer a vacant mask but full of life again — and the Teazer with a toss of his head is off on his spiralling sideways dance, the 'Oss snapping at the heart the dancer keeps just out of his reach all the time, the music of the big thumping drum and the piping squeeze-box striking up, and the Presenter, in his battered Ascot-grey topper and a plum-red face (probably they have all been drinking, Angela thinks), a greenish-black tailcoat buttoned tightly, and a cigarette stub pouted firmly in his lips as if to add to his cocky proudness, struts the way, baton in hand, to the next part of the town where the caracoling, plunging, prancing, heart-snapping horse must die, the eager crowd following, as the tides the moon.

> *Unite and unite and let us all unite,*
> *For summer is a-come unto day,*
> *And whither we are going we will all unite,*
> *In the merry morning of May.*

Angela looks round as she is carried along. The faces have filled with expression, enjoyment, that were still as the 'Oss when it died and emptied. There is a parson near her who wears a dog-collar and a thin linen jacket. He is young, with thick dark hair and a lean jaw of clerical cut. To her surprise she sees that his cheeks are wet, as if he had just been crying.

It is now well into hotel lunchtime. Angela feels a ravenous hunger. She has witnessed the death and resurrection of the great mask nine times. She has

94

been completely absorbed as if into another world: the turning twisting dance has put a twist into the ordinary world, and made it extraordinarily vivid. She sees each face and greets it in her mind as though it were a portrait that she recognised done by a painter who had caught the essential unity of each person. The *bang, bang* of the big and ancient Brenton drum fills her ears like a new heartbeat. She watches the dust twinkle in a sunbeam between houses and a small black boy who dances into it. She saw him join the crowd, pouting with surprise at first, but then he eased himself hesitantly into the music, his feet picking it up first, then his hips, as though it were travelling up his body from the ground, like a garment that put itself on him, and once it was over his shoulders he could move in the whole rhythm. She had seen his small black body in the short trousers and red jacket stomping and skipping ceremoniously between the white files of the practised Mayers; and now he dances by himself in a sunbeam. She slips out of the crowd along the straight street back to the hotel above which she notices her first-floor window presiding, passing the sleepers' car now empty and its windows unpearled of breath. Everything is new-minted to her eyes, and surprising. It is surprising but, by that, more itself: not the trigger or doorway to some road of fantasy like her father's images, which catch one up in a dance that wheels round and round no centre but himself alive and glittering and clever and the best, giving of its best. She finds herself wishing she could imagine him dead: it is impossible. On the hotel steps she is caught by the man-sized gilt letters pronouncing without stirring the hotel's name, and stands there marvelling. Behind her the music of the accordion and the thump of the drum rise out of the sunny town tirelessly as a heartbeat.

After a stodgy lunch she did not really want she felt as haggard as the great shifting dunes across the water. She sensed she had defiled herself by this meal; she used to feel this when she took Communion, that she should not mix God-food with house-food. Then when she shat the next morning she turned away from the toilet so as not to witness the defilement of God, on his way down to the sewers. She looked out at the sea: the dining-room window gave a wide view. 'The priest makes God who travels down the sewers into the sea, and from the sea into the clouds, and then down with the rain.' She remembers running out into a thunderstorm in her clothes and how it made her skin alive like sexual intercourse. She had been ashamed of doing this on an impulse, and wanting to do it each time it rained. She had confessed her feelings to her father, who told her to use hypnotic suggestion to get rid of any feeling she did not want. Later on, she got rid of a lover that way: she made herself feel nothing for him. This was the way she got her good degree: that and hypno-learning. 'But God was in the rain,' she thought as she watched the flashing sea, 'and I was God's lover in the rain. That dance would have made me fertile.' For she had eschewed lovers, and worked for her father after leaving Cambridge, and she was used to her dryness, her scanty moistures, her irregular emotions that burst out with her period and made her even more solitary on those days, scratchy and self-hating. She loved the dry brilliant fire of her researches on hypnotism.

God seems to have left the sun after that meal. The light looks thin and tattered on the waves, like old silk. The 'Oss is too powerful, she thinks, it is too powerful a suggestion, and I must rest and dream if possible to digest the impression. She goes upstairs and hangs the 'Do Not Disturb' notice on her door-handle, slips off her dress and bra, and lies down in her bed, between the clean sheets which, she is grateful to find, have been changed after her restless and sweaty night. The window is half-open, and the singing and music of the dance still comes up from the streets. She has the post-hypnotic suggestion from her father to sleep as soon as she has counted five and clicked her fingers, which she does. Immediately she is in a wide canyon of grey buildings which are so tall that they converge overhead so that nothing can be seen between them but a knife-blade of sunlight. There is no alteration in the music and drumbeat she hears, except that it echoes in the chasm of asphalt. As she stares about her she sees a shape like a pale ghost or slough come wafting sideways towards her from a great height. As it glides near, it bends nearly in half on some invisible waft of air, as though it were bowing with its back towards her. It is a cocoon of dust, the size of a horse. She looks up and down the street and sees several of these dirigible apparitions afloat and slowly descending and the flaccid rolling of others that have touched ground and lack the strength and opportunity of breeze or draught to raise them in their gliding vapid walk again.

The music is louder in the distance, with its thumping drum and its wheezing squeeze-box, and the toot of a little pipe too, but as she looks up and down the streets which converge to tall slots of shadow with their hairline sunlight above, she cannot see the source of the singing and playing. She is on the sidewalk near a large plate-glass window which is pearly with condensed moisture. She rubs the glass to look within, but the condensation is on the inside. There are shapes standing there that could be dress-dummies, and there is a hint of movement as though there were people in there too, but unless one of those people rubbed their breath away and she could see inside, she could not be sure.

About two hundred yards down the road a large crowd of people has appeared. They are milling round white dancing figures and a Teazer who holds out a white satin heart to a monster who is clothed in black and wheels and shines and shows a mouth full of bloody teeth from all the hearts he has eaten. As he swings, blood flies from his mouth and blooms on the white clothes of the dancers. The celebration moves closer and Angela sees George Frederick Pfoundes in his black psychiatrist's jacket and pin-striped trousers dancing in the place of the 'Oss, his mouth full of blood, his eyes glaring with hypnotism. His buttons glitter, and his brilliantined hair is swept up into tall plumes. As he dances sometimes his eyes are glaring and sometimes tight-shut, his face in repose as though he were asleep or dead, but dancing all the same. All the dancers are smiling and happy, but as she looks closer she sees that their eyes are glazed and they are in a hypnotic trance. It is the 'Oss, her father, who controls them! But then why cannot he snap the tit-bit off the end of the stick that the Teazer shows him, at which he runs, teeth bleeding, and is turned aside by the clever footwork at the last moment, like a bull with the muleta? She cannot see the Teazer's face, only the splashes on his clothes. Then he turns, and it is her face.

There is a parson in the surrounding crowd. He

reaches into his white linen jacket and takes a circular white biscuit from his pocket and munches it slowly. Blood runs down his chin over his dog-collar. Angela waves her hands in front of his eyes as he jigs along on his dance, but the eyes do not blink. She is very close to the centre now, to the whirling couple of Teazer and Father, but the faces turn and glare and sleep and glare without noticing her. She smells the breath of them both, and the heavy blood like chloroform on it. Is this smell the source of the hypnotism which keeps the audience in thrall? Will it overcome the Teazer before he can triumph? As she thinks this thought, the Teazer with a decisive gesture points his sceptre downwards towards the ground. With a dreadful hacking cough blood pours from her father's mouth, his legs crumple and he falls forward on to his hands, blood vomiting in a pool in front of him. His gaze has dropped from the Teazer, who stands without moving, still pointing downwards. Pfoundes now stares into the growing pool of blood. His face curls like burning paper and his clothes empty as the lapping pool grows. It steams a little, and his papery, empty eyes settle into it, their lids closing. The sun must now be directly overhead, because the long street suddenly turns golden. Angela steps into the blood, which has turned golden as sunlight.

And she wakes to a great shout of song from under her hotel bedroom window!

> *Unite and unite and let us all unite,*
> *For summer is a-come unto day,*
> *And whither we are going we will all unite,*
> *In the merry morning of May.*

It wakes her and the late red sunlight is on her

counterpane. She wants to join in, she wants to sing. She gets quickly out of bed over to the window, opens the lower sash and leans out. The 'Oss and his companions of the dance are just moving away up the long narrow street. Some youths catch sight of her and wave jeeringly and cover their eyes in mock horror, for she is bare to the waist, and doesn't care. The music comes rolling back up the street; there is a leathery little man beating the big drum slung from his shoulder. The thump of it makes her head swim a little. One dancing man, lantern-jawed and with a heavy stubble emphasised by his leanness and his white clothes, smiles up at her very sweetly and gently, while his feet beat out a ferocious rhythm in time to the drum.

A second wave of dizziness makes her think it prudent to withdraw from the window. Her pants feel wet and when she touches them there is dark red blood on her fingertips. Her period has come, and it is very copious, for the first time that she can remember. There is a relaxation inside her, which makes her glad, as if she had just cast off a burden. To go with that, the blood feels loose and clean, and she feels as if she can see it within, for there is a sensation of dark glistening. On an impulse she goes to the mirror and marks herself with a finger-dab of blood between the eyebrows, like a caste-mark. She reminds herself that she must not forget to wipe this off before she goes outside, 'Though I don't suppose the 'Oss would mind, with his great red eyes.'

She has put on a fresh skirt and a blouse in a glistening material, to match the feeling within. The sky is dark, and the street lamps are a warm yellow. The pubs have been open from four o'clock, and there is a slight restlessness among the crowds. Somebody strikes up with the 'Eton Boating Song', and a few voices join stragglingly. There are angry shouts against this and a strong Cornish voice cries out 'Keep the tradition! Keep the tradition!' An old lady hobbles away from the press in the street muttering 'Bloody furriners! Bloody furriners!' Anyone not born in the town is a 'foreigner' and those that 'break the tradition', as though this were a post-football jollification, are beyond the pale. Angela notices that the parson who seemed to be crying earlier on this morning is now an expert May dancer. He is capering adroitly near the inner circle close to the 'Oss, where the white-clad Padstow people are keeping the tradition. He dances accurately, but he keeps a respectful distance from the town-born dancers. He also has a professional air, for he is, after all, the representative of an evangelising religion visiting a conquered shrine. Ecumenicalism has, however, taught him good manners, and his eyes shine.

Most of the people in the street have now learnt the simple dance-step, so that the whole procession, headed by Presenter, Teazer and 'Oss, are dancing in unity through the town without the knots and snarls of crowding that made the morning difficult. How many dancers has the 'Oss worn out, Angela wonders; they must have replaced him many times, for the mask is still capering with undiminished energy. The lamps are whirling in his shiny gown like shooting stars and planets; he leads the people like the black crest of a flood with particles of white foam dancing on it. Angela finds herself very near the 'Oss: she is sideways to him as he lets the seven-foot hoop rear up, making him eight or

101

nine feet tall. A shudder takes hold of her, and the feeling of him spreads through her body, compounded of his capering image, the thump of his big drum, and the smells and vibrations of the crowd. She almost falls among the stamping feet, but a hand grips her arm, and a friendly face peers into hers. 'Please forgive me,' she says to the Cornishwoman in the white dress with its red sash streaking from shoulder to waist, and, 'Thank you very much.' The woman looks at her kindly and somehow, like the parson, with the hint of a professional air. Angela looks down and sees that the woman is pregnant, and understands that she is inspecting Angela for signs of this particular fellowship, which would account for the fainting. She has a broad, rather ugly face, like a Red Indian squaw, and her eyes are narrow and very sharp. 'It was — the beauty, you see . . .' mumbles Angela, and the woman nods. 'That's all right then,' she says, in broad Cornish. ''Ee's going to 'is bed now, my lover. Summer's in.' She lets go of her arm, and dances shuffling off into the crowd. Angela hopes that dancing is good for the baby.

> *One parting kiss I give thee,*
> *May nevermore behold thee*
> *I cannot bear to leave thee*
> *I go whate'er befalls me.*

That is the stabling song. The 'Oss and his company have come to the inn-yard where the mask is kept in one of the outhouses for most of the year. The crowd are singing to the 'Oss, who has drawn apart under the lintel. His Presenter and Teazer stand away from him on the fringes of the crowd, and sing to him with all the others. The great steeple-hatted disc stands tilted a little, as though listening with head cocked to his farewell. Suddenly the white-clad dancer has stepped from under the accoutrements of the 'Oss, the hat and mask are plucked off, and the hoop leaned against the wall. The man waits listening until the song is finished, the mournful, fond, unaccompanied voices. Many are reading from broadsheets that have been given away during the day.

> *Farewell, farewell, my own true love.*
> *Farewell, farewell, my own true love.*

As the notes die away the dancer picks the gear up unceremoniously, tucks the hat under his arm, and disappears with the hoop into the little outhouse. There is a deep sigh from the crowd — and then the people in it turn and begin to disperse. The great Hobgoblin 'Oss has been put to bed, in the Golden Inn stable where he is stored all empty during the year, separated into tarred cloth and wooden hoop, pole, hinge and decaying mask: 'Obb's 'Oss, Morris 'Oss, Robin's 'Oss, Holy Horse, Osiris Horse, the Devil himself. 'Satan, thank you,' says Angela to herself, very quietly as the parson strolls briskly by, on his way to a chaste bed.

* * *

'I'm dying, Angela.'
'No, Father. You'll be up and well long before ...'
'It's sad to let go. I had a dream last night. Persy came for me. She took me through the wall, but I don't remember what was there. The stone felt rigid and I couldn't see anything. I felt her hand in mine in the stone. I woke and felt this dreadful cold.'
'The doctor was quite cheerful about you.'

'I'm a doctor. He was cheerful for your benefit. I asked him straight. Don't cry, Angela. It's an adventure, you see. Angela! I have a plan.'

'A plan, Father?'

'I want you to do something with me. A last great experiment in hypnosis.'

'You mustn't get excited.'

'That doesn't matter now. Do you remember that story of Edgar Allan Poe's about hypnosis?'

' "The Facts in the Case of M. Valdemar". Yes, I should think I do. But that's horrible, Father. Do you want to keep alive by hypnosis?'

'Alive and paralysed for months, speaking to my hypnotist through a gaping blackened mouth, kept from decay by magnetic passes, and, woken, to crumble under my hypnotist's hands to a "nearly liquid mass of loathsome, of detestable putrescence" — no, my dear, nothing like that. Far, far bolder.'

'What, then?'

'My dear, I want to hypnotise you before I die.'

'Why, Father, why do that?'

'We're very close, aren't we?'

'As close as father and daughter have ever been.'

'Then you will be sorry to see me go. Don't cry.'

'Of course. Of course.'

'I want you to find out what has happened to me when I'm dead. I'm going to give you a post-hypnotic suggestion to search me out in the land of the dead.'

'How can I . . .'

'Hypnosis takes a person into strange worlds. Under hypnosis you can learn faster, sense deeper; you can control your body and mind, and you can open doors to new unexplored abilities. A poet becomes more of a poet, a scientist more of a scientist, and scientist and poet can find the qualities of

104

each other inside themselves. A spiritualistic medium becomes more sensitive to those vibrations that speak to her out of the other world, and which arrange themselves into faces and messages for those left behind. An ordinary person can become mediumistic; hypnosis can be the gate between the two worlds. I will tell you a secret phrase I have and that will be the password to assure you and the world too that the dead live; if I return and speak to you or if you find me in the place where I am then you shall know that it is I by this phrase. *L'anguille angoisse.* Repeat it.'

'*L'anguille angoisse.* Is it Racine?'

'Don't worry about what it means for the moment. I want you to set up the machine now. It will be my last experiment.'

* * *

Obit.

George Frederick Pfoundes. B. 1927. *Educ.* Tipton's and Cambridge. MB. BS. First class hons. PhD Manchester 1947 'Conscious Instinct and Self-Control'. MD London 1949 'Vascular changes in malignant tumours following on hypnosis'. DPhil. Cambridge 1951 'On the Proportion of Deep Trance Subjects in a Normal Urban Population'. Adviser, the Television Council, 1957, resigned 1963. Governor of the BBC since 1966. Director, Institute for Studies in Hypnosis, the University of Cornwall (An Cuntellow) since 1964. Publications include: 'The Induction of Hypnotic Trance by TV Watching: and its psychosomatic implications' 1963; 'The Red 'Flu: an epidemic explained as a consequence of hypnosis by TV programmes' 1964; 'Depression and

105

its psychosomatic sequalae associated with hypnosis under TV' 1965; 'Whither entertainment: Sound Radio and TV compared as health hazards' 1966; 'Hypnosis as an Educational Tool' 1967; 'The Pfoundes Biofeedback Oscilloscope: a method of deep trance induction using the cathode ray tube' 1968; 'Erotic Hypnosis: A Lovebook' 1968; 'The Handbook of Hypnosis' Ed. 6 vols 1969. *m* 1947 Persephone Lindqvist; one *d*.

* * *

'I want you to look for me when I am dead. I want to give you a post-hypnotic command to search for me. You will be able to see where my spirit is and what happens to me and you will be able to talk to me when I am dead. There will be no more mourning then. You will write a book to tell people what happens after death. That will turn a page of history that mankind has been struggling to turn since the beginning of time. You will search for me, search the world, search your mind, and when you have found me, I will speak through you and prove my survival by telling the world certain things that only a dead man could know. But we must do this now, Angela. Set up the machine.'

'Do we need the machine? I was in light trance as you spoke.'

'We need the deepest trance that any human being has yet undergone for this experiment. Do you remember the chain store magnate? I cured him of premature ejaculation. I couldn't stop him from coming in two minutes, but at least I could make it seem longer when I had taught him hypnosis with my Oscilloscope! It may be that the dead live faster than we do, streaking from molecule to molecule in their flux of changes. It may be that they live very slowly, like a mountain range. Hypnosis will enable you to travel these deeps, these accelerations in your human form. Set up the machine.'

'So that you can speak to me after you are dead.'

'So that I can speak to the world after I am dead. Listen to the hum of the machine, listen to the tunes of the machine, watch the improvisations of the tubes which are you yourself, depths in yourself as you approach the threshold of sleep and your eyes and your imagination are flickering like the machine but you are able to keep your eyes open and you are beginning to see pictures in the lights of the tube. Tell me what you see.'

'I see colours. I see landscapes streaming past as though I were in a railway train. Can you hear me, Father?'

'Your voice and the machine have harmonised; it is playing harmonics to your voice. You are speaking like a multitude. I can see your hands on the screen, your hands praying.'

'I see myself arriving at the University. Why, Father, they have put up a great stone statue to you. You are standing looking down at me from your stone face and you have a great stone book open in your hand. My footsteps take me round the statue to the great dark building with the door studded with nails. On the lintel in man-sized letters I see our name PFOUNDES. I try to open the door but the iron ring is too heavy. I bang on the door but it hurts my hands.'

'Come away from the museum, come back to the statue. Stare into the stone face. Look, the stone lids show a streak of darkness. They are lifting. There is no death! The stone statue is just a mask for my

107

death! Now you must search the stone for me. Feel as heavy as stone, as heavy as that stone statue. It must weigh a hundred tons! Your arms are stone, your shoulders are stone, your legs are stone. Lift your arm. You can do it in the instant before you become total stone. You must settle your pose. Your arm is a stone pillar. Lift it! Now it is stone and you are all stone until I say otherwise. Now you are stone you have nothing to do but to listen to me with your every crystal and your every fused particle, for you are all of a piece and have no seams or joints or bones through which my voice cannot go, or which might deflect my intention. You will be as a cliff or a mountain with my intention and nothing and nobody will turn you aside from it.'

* * *

'I am dying and when I die you will awake like a cliff or a mountain that can walk and think and you will execute my commands. You will enter into yourself and you will search for me, and you will search through the world for the place or the person where inner and outer meet and where I may reach you from the other world. You will commence your quest when I am dead and it is then that you will start to look for me, and you will find me and bring me back to speak to the world of the living. Nothing will stop you and you will experience no rest until you have found me and know my fate in the after-life and have communicated with me and I have spoken through you or until you know with certitude that I am unable to speak through you. You will never be free of me and you will search for my voice for ever, for ever, for evermore.'

* * *

'I think we should start the experiment, Father. That injection was dangerous in the first place and is not going to last for ever. When are you going to start? Do you want a nap first? Father? His head is deep in the pillow like a hood. It is as though he has turned to stone. His mouth is open. He has finished speaking. His tongue is quite dry. His forehead is cold as stone. How long have I sat here? There's the postman coming up the drive with the morning's letters! A new day! And the great hypnotist sleeps on in his death-bed. Can I wake him from his last trance? Here, Father, these are the passes you taught me. Over the forehead, down the face, over the chest. Wake up, it is time to wake up; you must speak to me. Ah, the skin is so cold. Here, I can wheel the machine to him, focus the microphones and cameras on him. What colours, what chirping sounds, like birdsong! Perhaps he is still alive, deep inside, perhaps his soul still flutters deep inside the flesh with its solid waxes. Father, speak. One word would release your soul. Whose soul would it release? Mine also. The screens are not giving their colours. There is a snatch of music like requiem from the quadrophonics. The screens have gone white, like folded linen.'

* * *

Have you seen him? she enquired of the rock steaming with rain. That way, into the crooked smoke? It was only a rock breathing mist out after the storm. But it beckoned, and inclined one way. I will go, as you suggest. His hypnotism was his jewellery. It sparked and sparkled. He put off his abilities. Van-

109

ished. Then she asked the fly. The fly trapped by her hands, dead in the muslin curtain. The fly told. A dead claw loosened. Pointed to the park. And pointed to the dunes. And the rain came again, pronouncing *sssss* and *t*. I completed the word, and by the stream enquired his whereabouts of an orange squad of creeping ladybirds. It wheeled. In that direction? Almost conclusive. With my stick I penetrated the bureaucracies of the ant-hill and obtained an answer. They ran for me in the ladybird direction. What better proof? Down the path towards the sand-dunes. Her voice scooped into them asking where? I heard the beating of a little drum, and www*here* they said. On to the wriggling toes of dune sand, up to the blown peaked shins, watching his expression blown in the sand, the turn of his neck here! the corner of his mouth there! the wind tramples over the colossus, smooths an eyelid under marram brows there! expression-dust everywhere! his mouth slithers under me and I fall into a dune valley which is his cupped hands. Speak, Father. Just one word and I can go home. All those thousands of ants pointing couldn't be wrong, could they? Those little stones are too small to speak. They do not have his face all the time. I will see that his face is unerased from a greater stone.

* * *

'Mr Protheroe, as trustee of the estate I'm sure you will agree that my father must have a suitable monument. The University, in whose cemetery he lies . . .'

'That would be the field of tumuli, near to the Museum of Cornish Archaeology, by the sand-dunes . . .?'

'The University has agreed to my erecting a suit-able monument over his grave. I have envisaged a portrait statue of him, one and a half life-sized, with his head turned alertly (you remember his way) and somehow *shining* . . .'

'Do you mean to illuminate the statue?'

'No, I'm looking for some wet-look technique about the hair, and the buttons. That new sculptor, Arroyo, does he do portraits?'

'I can find out, of course.'

'Very well. I want him with his head turned alertly looking up and across from a stone copy of the deluxe edition of his greatest book . . .'

'*The Pfoundes Oscilloscope*?'

'Exactly. His greatest book. The title must be clearly engraved and visible to the pilgrim looking up at the statue from below. The stone must be durable. Cornish granite. I want an exact portrait. We will select the page that we believe most relevant to his memory, and this must be photographed on an enduring metal plate and fastened in the stone book.'

'No one will be able to read it unless they climb up on to the statue.'

'God will see it.'

'And the birds.'

'I beg your pardon, Mr Protheroe.'

'I say God and the birds of the air, Miss Pfoundes.'

'The statue must be properly supported and must weigh no less than five tons. The university authorities have agreed to this. It will be the largest and heaviest stone monument in the cemetery, as befits the University's most distinguished and still most influ-ential alumnus.'

'That should keep him down.'

'Mr Protheroe?'

'Miss Pfoundes, I know you won't take this ill, but your father is dead. He is no longer influential. It is his books which are influential, and his invention, the Oscilloscope, from which you draw royalties. His hypnotic influence cannot extend from beyond the grave, Miss Pfoundes.'

'I don't see how you can be sure of that, Mr Protheroe. Are you trying to tell me that our money would be better spent than in this commemoration?'

'No, Miss Pfoundes.'

'No, Mr Protheroe.'

*   *   *

'The thudding of the Brenton drum and the pipe and wheeze of the squeeze-box brought me out to Father's statue. I think I catch the glint of his eyes between his stone lids in his immense silence. That stupid sculptor did not leave a gap between his lips, the mouth is sealed. How shall he speak to me, wearing this immense stone over the shoulders of his spirit? I can see his eyes, I will climb up on to his lap. No, the eyes have flown elsewhere, there are only two small dry stone cups in this statue. He has put this mask down. Sometimes he dances behind the shuffling mask of the dunes. I think now he has tunnelled deep into the old tumuli, as the rain leaches the flesh from his bones. I hope above all he will not wear his mask of decaying meat, or his bones, I could not love him, even here, among the dunes and the pines, under his white stone soul. Would he come to me, where the earth has eroded away from the ancient burial ground, and where you may sometimes find an old skeleton, light as a thorn-bush, rubbed into spikes by the sand? How long it will be before the dunes advance as far as the statue of George Frederick Pfoundes, and scour his skeleton into tumble-weed, to be blown along the seashore? This is the turfy shore of that sea, packed full of the bones of great men, all in their hypnotic trance of death awaiting the resurrection, the great statue floating high, like a moon over dry billows. I think of all the bones ground to sand of the old Cornish who made their encampments here and brought up their children and were buried in turn in their tumuli. With their magic, do they not still haunt the pines, ground to dust in the air, exhaling from the resinous pines that picked their broad faces? Why, the museum is full of the traces of them. Their flints and their beakers and their combs. It is dark here in the museum. I cannot risk using a flashlight. I have the key to the cases. I have marked my prizes.'

Angela Pfoundes lets herself back into the house in the pitch dark after moonset. She turns the lights on in the room in which her father died, and in which she acquired her compulsion. The Oscilloscope installation is still in place. Her skirt swishes because she is wet through. She finds she must do certain things before her compulsion takes imagery definite enough to follow. She must hear her guidance in a fitful sleep, as when the Brenton drum woke her tonight, and she looked out through the window and saw white-clad dancers disappearing into the dunes, her dream still with her. When she got to the university cemetery (and her father's statue is the magnet, especially after dark) she was nonplussed, but the little stream called to her with its voice and she lay down in it. The shock of cold water made her quite unfanciful for a few minutes, and she saw how mad she had become, and she wondered if she

113

could rid herself of her father's post-hypnotic command by consulting another practitioner, and she pulled herself together and began to get out of the water. But the feel of it shaping round her shoulders, and the glimmer of its currents that bent and wound below her feet as though her body were casting a long, twining, altering shadow deep along the water, brought her back into her trance. She had the key to the university museum of Cornish Archaeology, and earlier hints and fragments of hallucination had prepared her for her burglary. In the morning the strange burglary was announced by small wet footsteps, and the caretaker mopped them away before reporting the losses. He thought it was the Little Folk, as perhaps it was.

She had her stolen objects in a soft black satchel which she emptied on the table. There was a stone cup, hollowed out of a big flint. This had not been done, in the later stages anyway, by chipping and knapping, since the cup was perfectly smooth, its lip rounded, the interior deep and even. The pebble looked as though it had been scoured empty by centuries on the seashore, which more likely would have broken it. Angela held it up to the light, which shone through it, as if it were made of toffee-coloured glass. The base had been knapped almost straight, so that it sat up on the table with only a slight wobble.

The next object from the satchel was a crude comb carved from bone. It was square, and had four teeth, and the handle was rounded and bore on it a 'cup-mark': three concentric circles with at their centre a perforation in the bone, like an emblematic eye, wide open and staring. Angela had seen similar artefacts in Red Indian museums, and knew that they were called 'Cootie-combs' and the idea was to comb one's hair with them before sleeping, as this was supposed to bring powerful dreams. The American Indian ones usually bore an animal, who was a tribal ancestor, and the dream was said to bring him to have intercourse with the woman in her sleep, and that this would open her womb so that she would also be fertile by a human male. Thus every Indian in such tribes had two fathers. This one, from early Stone Age Cornwall, had only an eye, and Angela liked to think of it as the eye of dreams ever open in the darkness.

The third object was the frontal bones and orbits of an old skull. The bone had crumbled away, leaving only the low forehead with its jutting brows, and the two circles of the eye sockets joined by the bridge of the nose. It was like an elaborate spectacle-frame, a necroscope for seeing through the eyes of the dead. Angela took her booty to the big reclining chair in front of the tilted screens of the Oscilloscope, and switched it on with the remote control that lay on the padded arm. She opened a cupboard and took out a bottle of port, from which she filled the stone cup. She lay back in her wet clothes and pulled her hair free, so it lay over the chairback. She put the stony bone-face over her own, and lay back sipping the port from the hollow pebble, combing her long hair, and watching the Oscilloscope screens through the eye sockets of the Stone Age skull, which had settled very easily and firmly on her nose.

The speakers gave off their music improvised from the swishing of her skirt. She was as cold as a stone statue in her wet clothes, but this now assisted her detachment from her body. She thought at first she could kill herself to find her father, but then how could she communicate her finds? In her lack of care of herself, the irregular meals from tins, for she lived by herself in this house, the fitful sleeps, the carelessness to wind and weather, a detached, saner part of her mind had thought that she might catch a fever that would take her close to the borders of death where her father was, and enable her to report what she found there. This was no demonstration, however, and long practice of hypnosis had made her so healthy that her body was not easily susceptible to fevers, however she treated it. She lay combing her hair in the glassy music that the speakers gave off, the sensors in the chair responding to the coldness of her skin. Runs of tinkling notes responded to the passage of the bone comb through her hair. The screens still showed light-coloured pictures, as they had since her father's death, the image of which they had retained, and occasionally recapitulated. Pfoundes' dead face swam towards her in the screen, and the mouth opened and uttered hoarsely 'Search!' before it drifted sideways, and endless improvisations on the folding of tallow-coloured linens took its place. One day the image of Pfoundes would fade from the computer-memory, since the machine was built to be responsive to progressive hypnotism, to a developing course; meanwhile Angela found that it helped her reveries, and renewed the command. At first it had frightened her, especially because she seemed to detect the dark glint of a glance between the almost closed lids, but tonight her body was too close to the condition of the dead, in its coldness and with its dead spectacles, so that she felt the kinship and not the threat.

Now the screens darkened, or her reverie fading into dream did, and she saw instead of the steadily folding and unfolding grave-clothes, a rich total

116

blackness. It drew her forward and surrounded her; the speakers were sending out *silence:* this they had been designed to do on suitable occasions by emitting vibrations that were exactly out of phase with any sounds that might happen to be in the room, so that the latter were cancelled by wave-interference, and the area wrapped in soundlessness. In the silence she could hear an occasional clink as of a cooking utensil, and a muttered speech in some broad dialect she did not recognise. Suddenly on the screens all the stars came out in their thick constellations: it was like a frosty night and the screens were thickly set with large necklaces and clouds of stars, with studded shapes twinkling and pulsing. She caught her breath, even in her trance, with the beauty of it. Then the scene appeared to pan down on to an encampment. She could see the flicker of firelight, and the tall conical shapes of a narrow kind of tent. Bustling around the fires her vision caught glimpses of the broad-jawed, low-browed people. One of the women bending over a pot straightened herself and eased her back, staring into the screen full-face. Angela recalled the woman she had met at Padstow, who had stopped her falling among the trampling feet during her fainting-fit. The Oscilloscope microphones have been designed to pick up subvocalisations, and so for a moment the Stone Age Cornishwoman is immensely pregnant, and to the sound of a little pipe and a drum the 'Obby 'Oss peers over her shoulder, before Angela drifts away into sleep on the big red reclining chair, her clothes steaming as though she were burning with cold fire.

* * *

117

'Show me the room,' said Speaking Water. Angela had heard of spiritualistic mediums with Red Indian spirit-guides before — indeed, one in five of the professional mediums she had consulted received messages from the ghosts of Red Men — but a medium who was a Red Indian himself was new to her. She wondered who his guide was, who his chief communicator in the spirit world might be. Perhaps by some law of exchange and opposites it was a fat middle-class Cornishwoman!

She had seen plenty of these. She had sat in darkened halls while fast-talking clairvoyants pounced on members of the congregation with the information that behind them were standing Uncle Fred, or a tall woman in a raincoat, or suchlike. She had engaged these people privately for consultations, and had begun to understand the nature of the profession. These people were not like doctors — healers possessed of a certain body of knowledge which they could apply unfailingly and which was subject to scientific controls and verification. Rather, they were individuals elected by their congregations, to be responsive to those congregations' psychological needs by a kind of enhanced knowledge. That was on one level: the level of good advice and optimistic counselling. There was, she soon found, another level, which could not be explained so easily.

On one occasion she had been attending a 'service of clairvoyance' at a spiritualistic chapel at Petroc, not far from their home. The medium was a little wrinkled old man dressed in a blue anorak. He kept a tiny living dog nestling in the bosom of his coat during his entire — 'performance' Angela had called it at first; then, later, 'ministry'. There was a little ritual of calling and response that was gone through;

118

the clairvoyant up at the front of the hall, the congregation sitting a few steps below, down from the slightly-raised platform. The clairvoyant could thus see over the heads of the people in front of him, and could call on selected individuals. Behind him was a large carpet or tapestry hanging on the wall, depicting a bearded Jesus with staring eyes.

'You, in the third row, in the tan coat. I have a message for you.'

'God Bless You.'

'Listen, he says, you must go out in the month of March. Does that mean anything to you?'

'God Bless You.'

'Yes, now I see, it is a woman who has been ill a long time. She says be cheerful.'

'Thank you.'

'And she says she knows there have been drear times, but now the month of March is not far off they will change.'

'God Bless You.'

'Very well. Now I must speak to the lady in the white blouse at the back of the hall.'

'Thank you. God Bless You.'

'There is a darkness around you. You have had a great unhappiness.'

'God Bless You.'

'I see someone close to you. I see a bad winter.'

'My father died.'

'Yes, I can see that your father has died, but I cannot see him. I can see *silence* and darkness. A deep but dazzling darkness.'

So far this is guesswork, thought Angela, but I am not trying to test the man, I am trying to respond to the customs. Why else did I give him that information, that it was my father who was dead? It felt to

119

me that I wanted to help him to see further, to home in on what was so, in order that he could see more than I told him.

The clairvoyant looked bothered. The little dog gave a tiny yap and wriggled, the dog's master closed his eyes firmly and hummed to himself a bit.

'There's a white figure.'

Ghosts are often white, thought Angela, but she said 'Thank you.'

'But it's so cold . . .'

Not impressive, she thought. 'God Bless You.'

'There is someone who cannot move, but who is used to leading an active life, a very active bustling person.'

'God Bless You.'

'I see shining lights. Your father liked to use brilliantine on his hair.'

Angela felt faint. 'God Bless You', meaning, God Bless You with more sight.

'But now I see hair that is white and cold and does not shine. It is a statue.'

'Thank you.'

'There is a statue leaning over your shoulder, white as your blouse, as if growing out of your shoulder. Its lips are stone and cannot speak. It hums through closed lips like a television. It wishes it could speak. The face is like an eagle in anguish because it is stone.'

'God Bless You. God Bless You.'

But the other members of the congregation are restless. This is a bizarre communication, and not at all what they are accustomed to. They wish their respected clairvoyant would move on now, since he has given this lady some comfort; or if it is not comfortable to her, then that is probably her fault, since she looks well-off enough.

120

'The statue-face is veined with little cracks in the effort to speak. Young lady, good times are coming soon. Be assured of that. Now I want to speak to the man in the drill coat over on this side . . .'

After the meeting, Angela spoke to the clairvoyant. He cuddled his little dog while cups of tea were handed round.

'I was so grateful for what you said in the meeting. It gave me fresh hope. I wonder whether you would sit for me privately.'

'Young lady, I'm very glad that you got a message through my lips, but it's no use asking me about it because I can never remember what the spirits give me to say, and it's no use telling me about it because it's your life and not mine. I can't sit for you because my power comes in the meeting and nowhere else, and I wouldn't wish it otherwise, since people get comfort from what I say.'

'Thank you. I didn't understand that. God Bless You.'

'God Bless You.'

She moved away. As far as she was concerned, survival was proved. She did not see how the medium could have picked up *L'anguille angoisse* unless perhaps she had subvocalised it, though she did not remember thinking of the phrase, and it was unlikely that he could hear her across six rows of slightly fidgety people. In any case, she certainly had not subvocalised a whole description of Pfoundes' statue, his desire to communicate before he had died, nor how the hum of the Oscilloscope was rather like an inarticulate desire to communicate, and how it was also a kind of television set. Should she go back to him and ask whether he knew French?

She had brought several mediums to the house,

but once she explained the conditions, that she wanted them to submit to the Pfoundes Oscilloscope, they had all refused. She said that she wanted to hypnotise them because that was the essence of the experiment: hypnosis, especially by Oscilloscope, would increase their sensitivity as spirit-mediums, and if they needed no such assistance, then why was it that survival was still unproved and spiritualism, conceivably the most important human advance ever, if true, still a minority Christian splinter-group? One sensitive said she felt a chill in the house that would prevent her working, and advised Angela to leave. On another occasion she went to a medium in London with a reputation for materialisations. This she was convinced was a fake. The man knew who she was, and a big picture of Dr Pfoundes that she recognised from an old issue of *Paris-Match* duly appeared in a sort of haze over the table. It was quite flat, as if cut out. Angela thought that had she been less aware of the phenomena and conditions of hypnosis, she would have supplied the missing third dimension, and have thought that her father was there. The photo-face disappeared, to be replaced by a close-up of the statue-face. This *was* more solid. These people had done their homework, and could take 3D photos. Was that slight hum in the background from a laser, and the deathly-white face holography? The hum seemed to get louder, and her imagination made the lips tremble. A pulse came into the hum, as if somebody were trying to speak. I'm going under, she thought, and tried to see what was there. The image suddenly switched out and the medium in the red-lit darkness said 'Angela!' in her father's voice. Homework again, thought Angela, tapes of his broadcasts. And the side of her, a new side, the part of her that

122

seemed to see the point of an attitude of 'faith', said to her, 'This is like the spiritualist congregation, but more elaborate. You must assist the medium in his deceptions, in order that he may go beyond them, and see truth. What else is hypnosis but telling a person he or she is something, so often that they become that thing?' So she said 'Father' and the medium responded 'Angela . . . the dead live. The dead live in —' and then he broke off as the hum started and the faint white image gathered again over the table. The hum now came quite clearly from the medium's lips, and it was as though he could not speak when the statue had materialised its stone unmoving lips; but when the apparition was not there, then he could talk in Pfoundes' voice. Once again the statue faded, and the medium began 'Angela! the dead live, and they live in . . .' and as though the effort of speaking had brought back the statue, which was at the same time unable to move its lips, the voice ceased and the hum took its place.

This medium too had refused to submit himself to what she assured him were the enhancements of the Oscilloscope, and Angela now realised why. The 'homework' and the preliminary deceptions, the 'suggestions' to the client that the dead were present, which made them (apparently) appear, the presence of the congregation which enabled the clairvoyant to speak out, were all 'enhancements' of their own kind, like the Oscilloscope itself. Angela believed that the Oscilloscope was more powerful than any of these painfully evolved methods that the mediums used, and that once she found a medium willing to use it, then her quest would soon be finished.

Was her quest now nearing its end? She had found a medium who agreed to sit with the Pfoundes

Oscilloscope. She had heard of the medium Speaking Water — indeed, he was famous. He was an American Indian who had at first trained as a psychotherapist. In the annals of psychotherapy there are many accounts of mediumistic phenomena that have attended a powerfully afflicted patient's recovery. There was a famous quarrel between Sigmund Freud and his heir-apparent to the psychoanalytic movement, C. G. Jung, in which Jung had reported that the roof of his belly had seemed to him to glow like red-hot iron in answer to some remark of Freud's, and startling raps from the furniture had made their conversation inaudible. A big bookcase had split and toppled, and the two psychiatrists were compelled to finish their altercation out of doors.

Speaking Water was called John Ismay then, having taken the surname of the people who had adopted him after his rescue from the tenement fire in which his parents had perished. He had studied to become a doctor in America, and after qualifying had turned to psychotherapy. His hobby or spare-time study since he had understood his origins, had been Indian folklore, and he had seen that modern psychotherapy and the ritual practices of his forefathers converged. Much neurosis in modern people, it seemed to him, was caused by the lack of a rebirth ceremony at adolescence; the growing youngster approached this sudden appearance of his or her sexual powers quite unprepared, and when they came they aroused and rehearsed ancient traumas of childhood. The only thing to do was to go back to these early times of infancy — as indeed Freud had found — and confront these angry or demanding spirits.

This was what, in essence, was done on the analyst's couch: and in a successful analysis a rebirth of the

124

self was the result. John Ismay knew that American Indian cultures sent their adolescents out into the wilderness to fast and to build sweat-lodges in which the body was purified and cleansed as in a sauna, until it had gathered itself into its purpose sufficiently to yield up to its owner some precious revelation, some word or glimpse of his essential nature that would knit him into an individuality during the dangers and exigencies of his adult life. Often this came as a spirit communication, through the mouth of some animal. The young boy, lonely, having sauna'ed himself to a shadow, would be walking through the woods, for instance, looking for berries and bark-grubs to eat, and the wind would be waving the branches and making the wavelets choppy on the lake, when suddenly the whole scene would freeze: the branches would be stock still, the corrugated water would petrify to bone. Then on this still stage the only moving thing would be a solitary cloud in the blue stone sky, that would drift like a canoe of the ancestors until it was directly overhead, and rain on him and him only, and in the touch of the rain on his skin there would be words of import. Or it might be that a squirrel or a deer walked through those stony woods, and came up to the initiate, and spoke a new name for him, that was his name for the rest of his being, even in the after-life. John Ismay had gone out to the forests of the Adirondacks to repeat these ceremonies, hoping for nothing, for he was a fully-qualified thirty-five-year-old psychiatrist, but nevertheless when nearly dead from starvation, having thrown off all his pretensions and learning and sworn to the spirits of air and water to tear up his medical diploma, he had received his revelation. It was not a cloud that rained on him, but a great

125

quarter-moon that crept into the sky against the direction of the sun and hovered over his head. His skin became clammy with a silvery dew, and it was then that the gentle touch of water all over him, in psychotherapeutic terms no doubt a recapitulation of the feeling of the birth-waters of his mother, spoke to him. To him it was a spirit, the same water in infinitesimal drops as in the great sea. Accordingly he took the name of Speaking Water, and became a poet, and a student spiritualistic medium. It was clear to him that the visionary experience that poetry enacted, and psychiatry accepted as its principal healing force, and called 'insight', was to be lived. It was not to be confined to extremes of mental distress or (amounting to the same thing) the rigours of an Eng. Lit. course; it was to be made a way of life.

Angela knew that her father had many times tried to arrange a meeting with this man, and he had been carelessly evasive. He had been quoted by a journalist as saying that he was not interested in the superficial illusions of hypnotism, but rather by whatever it was that caused them. Once Pfoundes had reached him by phone, but when he announced who he was, Speaking Water simply laughed and rang off. Angela had never seen her father so still until the night he died.

Consequently Angela did not expect that her letters requesting a consultation and outlining its condition of hypnosis by the Oscilloscope would get much response. She was surprised when the phone rang and a deep voice said 'Speaking Water.' She had a vision of all the lips created by the wind over a lake speaking sibilantly. She agreed a time for him to call.

Angela had always distrusted people with huge faces. Now she realised that all the people she had met with enormous heads on the front of which were spread grimacing, over-reacting countenances, were people who also had small bodies. The head was a magnifying device for the body. Many actors were like this, since the face and head, like that of an earthworm, was their principal contact with their environment, so it was over-developed. Speaking Water had one of the largest faces she had ever seen; it was built on a grand scale. Fortunately the body was immense also, and so there was no impression of top-heaviness, nor any sense of the magnifying face full of momentary excitements dragging an unwilling and puny body behind it. He was more like a tree, with an immense trunk, and a great spreading countenance, like the leaves of a tree, sensitive to the winds of the air, but rooted in strength. Like a tree, it seemed to her he could be very still when the weather so occasioned, but if there were a storm around, his nature would participate. Nor would he run away; perhaps that was why one spoke of 'touching wood' because a tree could not run away from its fortune or misfortune, and it was a prayer for steadfastness without over-sensitivity. Angela felt stirrings in her which had nothing to do with spiritualism. She certainly wanted to touch this man, and did not believe that he would run away either. Perhaps the time would come when she was free of her other tasks, for she, like her father, could not afford to stand still, as yet.

That was the impression. In physical fact, Speaking Water, né John Ismay, was about six foot two inches tall, with broad, high shoulders. He wore his hair down to his shoulders; it was dark and heavy with a gloss on it: not the artificial brisk glittering of a brilliantined coiffure, but a natural sheen. He was in his forties, and solidly built but still very flat-bellied. He wore jeans, which covered rather high but strong buttocks, and a leather jacket with fringes on it. He saw Angela looking at the buckskin and the fringes, and he must have read her thoughts, or her face must have given too much away, because he fingered these and said, 'It's not corny if you remember that on Indian garments they represented pouring rain.' His jaw was large as her father's, the skin a dusky red colour, like a dark sandstone, the nose very long and straight. The brow was low and broad. The eyes were brilliant, dark as night. She felt those stirrings again, and he looked suddenly serious as though he felt them too. He put a hand on the doorhandle and made it look like doll's furniture. 'Is this the room?' he said.

'All the mediums I have met have been much smaller men. Small men with big faces,' she said.

'Would you have been more impressed if I had been small?' he asked.

'No, but I would have made allowances for you if you had not come up to scratch, and I can't make any allowances for so impressive a figure.'

'Thank you very much. I shall try to make no mistakes. For one thing, I shan't take a fee for whatever I do in this house.'

'But you should. The estate is very well off. The announcement I propose will make a lot of money too, since the media will be involved.'

'Are you quite sure what that announcement will contain?'

'Yes, of course. It is the Good News. The Dead Live.'

'Have you thought that they may not be happy?'

'I'm sure my father's ghost will be happy when he has completed his life's purpose in death.'

'Did you not think that there might be a Heaven and a Hell and a Purgatory also?'

'I'm sure there will be enlightenment in the after-life, and we shall all understand our sins.'

'Perhaps we shall not want to be rid of our old, comfortable sins. Perhaps a sin is a habit that will keep us from enjoying the after-life, which will seem a Hell to us. I will not take your fee for what I do in this house, because I shall enjoy doing it. There is something very cold here that I wish to warm. First I want to warm it with my body.'

'I can't understand you. Do you want the fire on? No, I see . . . your presence . . . what do you mean, for God's sake?'

'Well, I saw it in your face. You know what is coming. It's something you've not done yet. Look at my hand.' He spread out his hand and stretched it out in front of her. It was hard and muscular, and it was deeply and simply lined, like the pad of an animal, the palm of a monkey. 'Do you see the rails on which my life runs?'

She pored over the lines. 'What is this?' tracing out one of them, and that quiver had returned.

'It is you,' he said, 'and look where it joins.'

The hand came out and laid on her shoulder, very dusky red like a wine splash on her white blouse. His face bent down on hers and kissed her hard, the big features filling the universe. The quiver in her belly had become a twining of appetite, an empti-ness that cramped and pulled because it wanted to be filled. His hand was on her hip now, and she was held in the small of her back with a firmness she

129

thought could have swung her up to the ceiling. She remembered the high buttocks, and how they were exactly developed for the thrusting that now she knew was inevitable and which she welcomed.

The hand that stroked her hips was now under her skirt and her pants and exploring her bare skin. It came round to the front and rested on the moist bush. A finger found her special place, and gently began to twirl the little sensitive knot of tissue. She had become very wet and warm there, and warmth was spreading through the lower part of her body in a way that she had not experienced before, like straight whisky glowing in the stomach, but lower down, and infinitely comforting. The glow spread up the small of her back and across her shoulders. He carried her across to the reclining chair which was the focus of the Pfoundes Oscilloscope. 'Wait!' she cried out, 'that is the machine.' 'You wanted me to perform with the aid of the machine, Angela!' and he studied the switches on the armrest. The machine hummed into life and the screens flickered. John Speaking Water eased out of his trousers, and gently broke the cloth in the crotch of her pants. His warm self entered her and produced more warmths that shot through her and at once she felt herself coming as though her belly were panting and drawing in great gasps of healing air, as though her lower body had run a race and was now drawing breath in lovely sighs, as though a membrane had broken and new lungs full of life-giving blood were in operation. She saw lights behind her closed eyelids and opened them into a hush. The Oscilloscope speakers were beating out silence and on the screens she could see no fanciful improvisations, but simply the bare buttocks of a large red man covering her in her

130

father's reclining chair in the room where he had died.

The chair was a little wider than an ordinary single bed, but this was not commodious enough to allow Ismay's great frame to do more than ease on its side, holding her close to him. The Oscilloscope still refused to improvise. She would have expected toccatas and choral climaxes, and pictures of fireworks and Indian sculpture or roaring furnaces, but all the screens gave back, like mirrors, was the plain sight of the two people resting after love. The silence that beat out from the speaker exactly matched the peace in her head and the peace in her body, particularly her skin, which felt as though it were open, as though it had no surface, since it had lost all its tension and its wayward conflicting electricities. It was probably the electrical silence of her skin that the speakers were responding to — she knew the chair's surface was designed to detect and monitor these electrical changes — but here evidently there was no vulgar electrical sprite present for the machine to make a monkey of and turn her into a petrified contemplator of some small disagreement of herself within herself, taking the small anxiety for the whole, and hypnotising her with it. Was that all that there was to her father's life's work? Mere anxiety? Did he hypnotise all those people by magnifying their anxieties so they couldn't move, and face to face with them would do anything they were told in order to rid themselves of them? Was that really all? And this last experiment of the Great Hypnotist, was that only to frighten people with their greatest anxiety of all? She saw the screens change as these worries slipped back into her mind, altering her tensions, her skin-currents, and the white stone head of Pfoundes appeared seen from behind, the picture slowly moving round and making the head seem to turn towards her.

'Is this your great machine then?' said John, still holding her. 'Ah, I recognise your father. He has just come back into your mind. You know that all this apparatus does is to magnify your own thought-forms, or mine. Look.' The statue nodded its head, and faded. The camera panned to the pine trees beyond the cemetery, on the edge of the dunes. John Ismay appeared walking through, treading the pine-needles, and raised his hand in greeting. He wore only a loin-cloth, and his body had a sheen on it, as though it had been oiled. As he stood there, the scene darkened, and the sky came out in stars. Firelight appeared, and the bustling, low-browed, skin-clad people. The pregnant woman scouring the pot appeared once again, and raised her head, and smiled out of the screen. Ismay stepped forward into the picture and laid his arm round her shoulder, as if to say 'She is carrying our child.' A faint rushing, as of distant horses' hooves galloping nearer but still very fast and faint, came out of the speakers.

The pictures had been so vivid, that Angela was really quite surprised to turn and realise that she was still on the couch, fully-dressed except for the crotch of her knickers, with the Red Indian spirit medium who had removed his trousers in order to make love to her. It had been a seance indeed, but not part of the arrangement. Was it included in his fee? Then she remembered that he had explicitly disclaimed his fee for anything he might do in this house, which he said he was sure of enjoying. She felt that she did not want to go on with the spiritualistic seance that she had promoted. All the arrangements were made, the journalists probably on the night-train, and the television cameras would arrive next morning. Yet she felt that her father's questions had been answered, though not explicitly. It was strange: you had to be careful with hypnosis; it was apt to act more literally than you might have wished. It was like the three wishes in the fairy-tale. You had to be very careful how you phrased them. You might ask for the wrong thing. She herself had been near suicide, because it was the most direct way of joining her father, and had her post-hypnotic command not enjoined her to make his communication to the world, then she would undoubtedly have killed herself as a result of it. She had known ludicrous instances of a hypnotic command being received too literally, as though the responsive psyche awakened by the hypnotic techniques were as innocent and willing as a child: there was a famous instance sometimes quoted in the text-books, of her father being stung by a wasp at an important hypno-medical congress, and all the delegates being enjoined to defecate as a result. In her case, the command had been to prove 'survival' and now she felt the important element of that was that *she* should prove survival of her father's death, and the medium had done that by awakening her to sex in a manner which her perfunctory undergraduate encounters had not prepared her for. She was a survivor now, indeed; and, moreover, she had seen a dreadful sham in the famous Pfoundes Oscilloscope. The truth was given by this other 'little machine' protected by a warm bush and with an excellent small switch that never failed: the images and sensations that this gave were truth, being given through the body; the Pfoundes Oscilloscope was a mere *farceur*.

'Oh, must we go on with this sham of a press

133

demonstration now?'

'You wanted to prove survival. What we did is the gateway to life, but you can't expect a mechanised age to see that. Perhaps our demonstration may turn up something that looks better for people than your excellent father could have intended.'

'Caught in his awful machine, you mean.'

'I wasn't meaning to be unpleasant about your father — but, yes. Let's be kind, though. It's only because it's misused that it's such a monster. It's a simpleton really, as most machines are, and makes people look a bit idiotic unless they use it with care. You know, it's like Faust and the Devil, and another way of getting your wishes granted. Faust would have been quite safe if he hadn't conjured up the Earth Spirit and told her she was ugly. The ugliness was his, separate from the Earth Spirit. It was after that the dog Stinker, Mephistopheles, appeared. This machine is full of the Earth Spirit, metal from the Earth quickened by the Earth's electricity. So do not tell her she is ugly, please; or if you do, accept the consequences. Look, it works quite simply.'

And again he showed her, but this time the barrier between herself and what the screens showed seemed to have gone, and she was walking with him through the pine woods, and could hear the soughing of wind in the needles above, and smell the resin on the air, just as she felt his hand holding her arm. They walked towards the site of the statue in the cemetery, and there was a light shower through the pines as they walked that wetted her shoulders a little. Then they came to where the statue should have been, but there was instead a village of skin tents, and people with low broad brows who greeted Ismay with great friendliness, smiling at her. They came to the preg-

134

nant woman scouring the pot, who looked up from her work and put it down and stepped towards them; John put his arms round both women's shoulders. Angela found herself wanting to kiss the long-dead woman who was so much alive, smiling and nodding her head with its dark coarse hair and big jaws, rather like a friendly ape — no, that was condescending of her — the woman had more animal nature than the modern women Angela had met, and this gave her an immediacy and presence that these others lacked. There was no reservation about this young woman, she did not withdraw, she was open and expectant, and her eyes were bright with the enjoyment of the world and herself and, indeed, Angela. Yet she had died a million years ago.

'Is this your wife, John?'

'No, Angela. It is yourself.'

'I can't understand you! Myself?' She turned abruptly towards him, and they were in her father's downstairs workroom again.

Ismay looked down from his height, and seeing that she was upset, drew her down to sit on the couch again. 'What did you see then?'

'I saw a million-year-old ghost, who was like a woman I met once at Padstow. Is this your mediumship? Can you call up spirits on these panels?'

'All I did was to take you to where your father's statue is, in your imagination, with the aid of these screens. Then I withdrew, and let your own self continue. I don't say "mediumship". I want it to be a "ministry".'

'I can see my father never truly knew how to use this machine. He was a tyrant!' And she began to sob, and pouring rain showed on the screen, and the sound of rain came out of the speakers. Like the prow of a white ship, the Pfoundes statue-face came nosing through the rain, tears of rain pouring down its cheeks.

'Angela! Is that the first time you've cried since your father died?'

'Yes, oh yes.'

'Let it come then. Look, I am crying with you.' Tears poured out of his eyes and she remembered her first impression of him, that he was like a tree, in which the weathers were embodied. The screens showed nothing, not even reflections of the real face she saw in front of her, weeping not for her, but with her, and the speakers gave no improvisations or echoes of the fall of their tears, but remained mute, like sympathetic servants at a family funeral.

'Let me show you how easy it is to master this machine, Angela. It has been the master of your life, under your father, and it has magnified his personality to you so that even now you will not understand his dead wishes if you receive them. Indeed, the machine destroyed your father by magnifying him, and he will only survive as a spirit in his inmost core, the unchanged, undissipated part, the part that was not destroyed by being seen so large and energetic. You, all innocently, were part of this machinery of destruction of this man, for, by loving him, you helped the machine to magnify him. Now you should see what you allowed to happen, by becoming the mistress of your father's invention. Look — it's so simple — these are balanced circuits, and they wobble and oscillate together, picking up all the unconscious language you do not know you are expressing, gesture, smell, skin-colour, skin-potential, muscle-tone. Any of these can over-ride any of the others, but the chief portal and instrument of this great display is your unspoken words.'

'Can it read minds?'

'Of course not! You forget. It can hear your subvocalisations. It can hear the thoughts you speak under your breath without knowing it. Know it, and you can begin to control it. Look. I will speak my name aloud. JOHN, JOHN SPEAKING WATER.'

The screens leapt into jagged life. John had shouted his name, he had cried it out, and the response of the machine was thunder and lightning; a violent oscillation that shook the room as the audios gave out peals of thunderclaps with great echoes, underlined with blocks of silence; the screens showed violent alternations of black and white as the echoes rolled round the room and Angela put her hands to her ears and the howlback built up and up, the machine responding to the loud noises by making louder noises still which fed back into the machine to produce loud noise — Angela rushed forward and turned the 'Off' switch on the chair's armrest.

'That would have destroyed the Oscilloscope. Beyond a limit the microphones do not cut out. My father used this to demonstrate intolerable sound to blind men. He used it to demonstrate the intolerance, and to get control!' She started laughing. 'I should have let the bloody thing bust its guts,' she said.

'Well, then we would have had to send all those newspaper and television men back again,' said John. 'Let me show you now how to make pictures on the screens,' and he ceased talking and closed his lips. She saw his Adam's apple moving, and realised that he was speaking under his breath, he was saying his name quietly, in a still voice, very quietly and very deeply. On the screens appeared

137

the vision that she had seen when he had announced his name over the telephone, her vision of a lake full of wavelets all speaking the one word in a still small voice, a word fashioned on the water by the wind made by the world spinning in space, the word it uttered from its place in the heavens, written in one of its forms on an open expanse of water surrounded by trees that were showing in their swaying and the openings and closings of their canopies the same word played on their natures also. The machine now put John's name up in computer-script on the screen.

'When you see that,' he said aloud, 'you know you have cleared its circuits right down to basic requirements, and it will keep steady, and show exactly what you tell it to, within the limits of its computer's store of information, of course, which it is adding to all the time.'

'You could have faked a magnificent seance, knowing all this. You could have put up the biggest fake of all time, and convinced the world of your religion. You could have shown us exactly what you pleased on this machine, while we, poor idiots, used it merely for wallowing in. You could have made us all sheep by the terrific pictures you could have put on. Why didn't you? Or do you want me to help you be a fake medium, and we show the world what we want them to see? Is that your intention, John? I would go along with that, if it was a secret between us. It would have to be, wouldn't it. Is that what you intended?'

'No, of course not. I wanted you to know what you were doing. I want you to have free will, which is what I want for myself.'

'When did you learn about the Pfoundes Oscilloscope? Did you have to decide not to take us for a ride when you understood it?'

'I knew nothing about it until I came into the room.'

'You knew all about it as soon as you saw it, I suppose?'

'No, Angela, I only understood it after we had made love together.'

* * *

The caterer's men had brought a lot of little gilt chairs with red seats which they arranged in rows facing the end of the room where the Oscilloscope and the Oscilloscope's reclining chair stood. One of the men was in the van outside superintending the crushing of ice and the spreading of relishes; the other, who had donned a pair of immaculate white cotton gloves, was serving, from behind a white-clothed trestle table, glasses of whisky and canapés. The sun shone through the broad windows opening on to the lawn all down the one side of the room; and the effect was more that of a wedding reception than a seance. An aisle had been left in the rows of chairs on the left-hand side of the room, by the bookcases, and a space in front of the chairs so that they were well distanced from the Oscilloscope and its couch; a large upright chair which supported a frame of wires on which curtains ran; and a table bearing a tambourine and a tall speaking-trumpet like the steeple-hat of the 'Obby 'Oss. This aisle and front space was for the television cameramen to walk up and down in with their shoulder-supported cameras and their directional microphones.

The journalists were not dressed for a wedding

reception, nor did they seem particularly untidy people. They were mostly young, and many of them were women, including one who was very obviously pregnant. She was dressed rather as if for a wedding, with a flowery frock and a white floppy hat. Most of the other women wore jeans. The editorial brief seemed an incredible one: all had been told that a famous Red Indian medium guaranteed a materialisation of the ghost of a famous hypnotist, and that he was being paid a record fee for this out of the millions belonging to the Pfoundes estate. The word was that 'no materialisation, no fee' had been agreed; and this meant at the very least a most interesting and discussable fiasco; at best the ghost of an eminent man would walk among them, proclaiming the millennium of a religion that promised life after death. The Chairman and President of the Magical Circle were there; and a Derby and Joan couple who represented the spiritualist churches of the country. These mingled with representatives of the quality women's magazines, who were interested in Angela's story, if her father managed to distinguish himself after death; of the Sunday supplements with their photographers elaborately festooned in motor-wound cameras and other paraphernalia; and the daily tabloids who were hoping to unearth the sexual angle: possibly a liaison between Angela and the medium, who knows; or sex-life among the ghosts — eighteen posthumous lays I have known, by George Frederick Pfoundes. The excitement was subdued, since nobody really thought anything would happen, but the room was quite tense: there was a shriek and a round of applause when the caterer's man slipped on a smoked salmon sandwich that had dropped from somebody's plate, and nearly went flying with a tray of drinks, saving himself and the whisky with phenomenal dexterity, his dazzling smile also intact.

Angela had been greatly reassured by John Speaking Water's demonstration of his power over the machine that had ruled her life nearly as long as she could remember. He warned her that though the machine was now under their conscious control, and would reveal only what they commanded, unless they desired otherwise, this did not mean that Angela's quest was over, or that she was not in any danger. He told her that the machine certainly magnified what its users unconsciously experienced, but that because Angela unconsciously experienced her father in her mind, and the machine showed his images, this did not mean that her father was only in her mind.

'There is a very powerful intellect somewhere both in you and outside, despairing, wild, that resembles your father, but who has been terribly altered by the distorting effects of his machine, by his using it over and over to change himself through his adult life, who is going to try and justify himself, and impose his will on the world, through the medium of my own skills, and through the media men and women who are in that room downstairs, waiting, like the Pfoundes Oscilloscope, to change and alter the world by reflecting it in their machinery of communication, to add a little bit here, subtract something there, pull it a little towards policy there, push back a little that might offend the advertisers there, but all much, much larger than life-size, in the whispering print and in the hollering photographs. Your father will come back if he can, and you know he has reached at you not only through me, but through the other mediums you have consulted.

141

You know he has reached at you through your own depths, where his continued imprint has solidified into a statue more powerful than any man.'

'Not more powerful than loving you.'

'No, but planted firmly on that ground.'

Angela could feel the electricity in the house. She brushed her hair, and her clothes crackled and sparked. The feathers in the duvet rustled and humped it as she walked past — she was impatient with that and took it up and shook it out violently, and this dissipated the charge, and it lay quiet on her bed. There was a mysterious white dust in her shoes which she thought was spilled facepowder, but it was gritty when she shook it out into the wastepaper basket. She peered at herself in the little mirror above the handbasin and her face abruptly went lopsided and she grasped her cheek with a gasp. The mirror had split across and one half of it dropped with a hard crash into the basin. The reflection of her from the remaining half looked white as a statue-face smashed with a hammer. She knew the thought-forms of her father were crowding into her mind, and that if she were in the space presided over by the Oscilloscope they would reveal themselves on the screen and the speakers: and it was planned that she should join with John in the attempt at materialisation. She was confident that there was no danger of a fiasco from her panic-stricken thought-forms alone, which, John explained, were the attempt of her mind *not* to allow a true communication through, by splitting it up into obsessive and accustomed images. She was afraid of what the true ghost would say, so she split it up into many fanciful ones, he told her. This was the reason why the materialisation medium she had first consulted had picked up from her (for most mediums worked like the Oscilloscope itself) a man who could only be seen as a statue with sealed lips, or be heard as a voice that could not complete its message unless seen. There was no reason why the image of the statue could not have spoken, except her own fear. Now in the bathroom the shower-curtains rustled like rain, and a draught blew up the waste-pipe with an unnerving wail. Impatiently she drew the curtains, finding nothing untoward, tucked them into their loops, and poured a little disinfectant into the waste-pipe.

John was waiting for her on the landing, looking inscrutable, still dressed in his fringed jacket and jeans. Hand in hand they went downstairs towards the waiting ordeal or triumph. Into the big room full of gilt chairs, where her father had died nearly a year ago, and where she had received her final instructions, past the banks of flickering television monitors, down the side-aisle in which the television cameramen stood aside for them. Angela sat in the curtained upright chair, while John stood and addressed the audience.

He explained how the Pfoundes Oscilloscope was a device for magnifying our unconscious reactions, and playing them back for us to see, so we could co-operate with them. He explained how the chief focus of the machine was in the front of the room where he and Angela would be, but that cameras and sensors throughout the company would pick up and throw on to the screens and speakers corporate phenomena of the audience so that they would be participating also. 'There may,' he said, 'be among you a particularly gifted spirit medium whose extra power and intervention could be the deciding factor in our success tonight. Always and

143

everywhere spiritualism has been a matter of everyday people joining together to magnify their gifts
into one bigger talent: in what happens today it
will not be the triumph of a single person that is
significant, for that person is only elected to be the
channel of a common faculty present in greater or
lesser degree in all of us. The Oscilloscope will aid
us in making that faculty visible to us as a collective
awareness. The ushers will now pass round the
cards, please.' The caterer's men with their white
gloves and white coats were now passing along the
rows packs of large stiff cards on which were pasted
an assortment of photographs of G.F. Pfoundes; pos-
ing by his Oscilloscope — a first model — in a long drab
coat and early Cary Grant spectacles; receiving his
BA at Cambridge, dressed in rabbit fur and bands
with a sheepish infant's face; sky-clad, that is, naked,
posed for their witch-wedding with Angela's mother
and Angela inside the big domed belly of the pregnant
witch, the goat-masked priest offering them the
silver cup on their knees; as a baby on a rug; receiving
his PhD in a very stiff collar with a very tight white
bow; posed benevolently unsmiling in his consulting-
room behind his shiny desk, his hair and buttons
sparkling in the photographic lights; and as a statue
photographed dark against a blanched sky, and
floodlit white at night.

'This, ladies and gentlemen, is the subject, and it
would be helpful to us all if you used them to keep
his image firmly in your thoughts during the experiment.' This passing of her father's image among all
these strangers irritated Angela more than she could
allow herself to show, though she knew it was desir-
able, particularly as a counterforce to her own
imaginings of him, obsessed by his posthumous

144

command. The caterer's man let down a large poster of Pfoundes from the picture-rail of the wall opposite, and her father stared straight into Angela's eyes down the length of the room. It was a close-up, blown up, of the consulting-room photograph, and he wore all his professional aura of competence and power.

Could she control her own thought-forms, for John was now turning on the Oscilloscope? He had taught her that subvocalisation was the key to control, and now all her lost impulse to prayer came back to her. Her father was now truly dead, so that any bad wish she found in her prayers for him could no longer do him harm; therefore her prayers could only do good, whatever happened, and she found that a floodgate had burst within her, and it was love for him. Sheer love and pity for this obsessed man who had wished good as he saw it for people, and cured many, but in his own image. So many of his patients had wanted to become hypnotists, just like him! Some had, and had helped him build variants of the Oscilloscope. Others had found new gifts within themselves using his methods, and had changed utterly, and gone beyond her ken. Now her prayers had turned to a sort of song under her breath for the soul of this man, and a song that asked forgiveness for herself. Her task had been, she saw, to become herself and not his. It had been her evil as much as his to accept the post-hypnotic and post-humous suggestion that had led to this instant; she should have refused, and long before that have lived her own life, and danced all night, and fucked all comers, instead of becoming ministering Angela to a great glittering phallic phantom, with shiny buttons.

John had turned on the Oscilloscope. The picture that had formed on the main screen directly facing

145

the audience was an identical copy of the wall-poster that stared back at it from the rear of the room. This picture travelled through the television camera lenses and appeared on the small monitors at the back of the hall, which was of course also scanned by the Oscilloscope cameras, as all the room was. This meant that the pictures in the two sets of machinery, Oscilloscope and TV equipment, were staring at each other, and gradually adjusting and redefining each other through each other's equipment. This had the effect of causing the image to, apparently, play with its face. A block of shadow to one side flattened the nose, and two spots of hectic hue appeared on the cheeks and burned there violently like small suns before they winked out. The balls of the eyes twitched this way and that, skittering so fast and so wittily that the people sitting there began to laugh. Then they held still and the irises came nearer and began to revolve in spirals, drawing people's gaze inward, along an apparently endless corridor, as in a hypnotic sleep. It was natural that the eyes of the Great Hypnotist should contrive to revolve in this fashion and several people dropped off. Angela was terrified. None of this was planned or expected, yet it bore the marks of coercion, and she remembered how Pfoundes would joke as he set up the 'hypnoscope', which was merely a card like a gramophone record painted with a spiral, for an audience, and catch them off their guard before turning the handle that twirled the spiral down down down into sleep for the more suggestible ones. He was doing this now from beyond the grave, or someone was, she did not think she could be blamed. Now the nose lengthened like a snake, and wove hypnotically from side to side, and the firm

146

professional mouth bagged down over its jaw and the jaw slowly lowered like a drawbridge onto a deep gullet-blackness at the end of which was a spot of light like the opening of the other end of a tunnel that was slowly rushing towards them. Out of the speaker came the regular tap of a brush on a drum, sibilant and insistent.

John had not counted on the feedback effect of the television cameras enhancing the powers of the Oscilloscope; he blessed his ancestors that the programme was being recorded and not televised live over the country; that would have released powers indeed. As it was he saw a serious situation developing as eyes fixed and jaws sagged among the rows of chairs and he clasped his hands and threw his head back and prayed as hard as he could. He supposed he should turn the machine off and start again, but he wanted to co-operate with the phenomena and bring them to an issue, not to quench them. The tunnel-ends on the facing screens were careering towards each other, and the hair of what remained of the gaping face was bristling upright so that it seemed surrounded with a black sunburst, the eyes still staring and revolving. Then the feedback effect became too much for the image, some mistake had been made by the power that controlled it, and it had gone a little too far in one direction or another, the light at the end of the tunnel a scrap too bright, perhaps, and it suddenly darkened and the mouth grew bright, the whole picture solarised into negative and winked out. John clasped his hands tighter and prayed harder and his prayers appeared as computer-script on the screen: GREAT SPIRIT MASTER OF THUNDER AND WATER HOVER OVER THIS COMPANY AND UNITE THEM TO OFFER UP

147

THEIR HUMANITY TO THY ERRING SON G. F. PFOUNDES AND IN THE NAME OF THE GREAT SPIRIT AND FOR ALL THE GODS' SAKE TURN THE CAMERAS AWAY FROM THE SCREEN OR WE SHALL ALL BE PARALYSED. The cameramen in the aisle broke out of their trance and put their apparatus down on the floor. One of them turned both turret-heads towards the wall: he was sweating from some fancy he had encountered in his trance, and understood the dangers. The other remonstrated with him — how were they able to get their story without filming it?

The slow brush-strokes on the drum that had been coming from the speakers in a compelling rhythm now broke into a faster beat, that was like the galloping of distant hooves. The screens remained blank. Angela had expected John to sit down in her stead in the materialisation cabinet — that is, the curtained chair — and go into his trance once the preliminaries were over; however, the strong spirit of G. F. Pfoundes had opened the battle with a skirmish that had nearly become a massacre. The preliminaries had nearly been the end of the affair. Surely John would sit in the cabinet now and have the window-curtains drawn, and the curtains round his chair drawn, and empty himself of his own spirit behind them so that Pfoundes might be drawn into a materialisation, and questioned, and accomplish his purpose, and go to rest, and perhaps a better world would dawn out of his mistakes and his agony. Angela got up out of the big upright throne and motioned John towards it. 'No, you are the medium now.' The noise of hoofbeats came more strongly though still distant through the speakers, and then silvery laughter, that was contemptuous and fond. The screens went quite blank, then jet-black. Stars broke out over them, and the image panned across the constellations, then dipped and showed the Pfoundes statue on the skyline. The audience braced itself for a further assault. Along the path towards the statue, through the cemetery's formal gardens, walked a dark figure. The light from a quarter-moon broke through and illuminated it as it reached the statue's base. It was the wide-jawed, low-browed Cornishwoman of the ancient encampment. Her belly was like the dome of Silbury Hill, in the skins that she wore. The camera flew closer, and she laughed into it, contemptuous and fond. She held up her finger in an attitude that swiftly had become admonitory and ghostly. She said in the small clear voice of the laughter: 'He is not born yet.' The camera caught her upraised finger. Angela on the medium's chair was in deep trance, her eyes fast shut, and she moaned through closed lips. As the Cornishwoman on the Oscilloscope raised her finger — cause or effect? — Angela raised hers in a similar attitude. The camera held the image of the finger, and caught it as it swooped down and the woman pointed to her mountainous belly. 'He is not born yet,' she said again. Angela's eyes snapped open and she stared at the Cornishwoman's image on the screen. Both women pointed to their bellies, and both laughed fondly and contemptuously. The sound of soft galloping hooves nearing grew very loud. The audience swears that at this point the women stepped towards each other and embraced, yet how could they, one of them only being an image made of light and metal?

The screen darkened again, and one star appeared, rushing towards them, with the sound of foetal heartbeats. Inside the star was the statue of Pfoundes, reading his stone book. As they watched, the statue attempted to turn over the next page in his stone book. Its fingers grappled with the sculpted pages, and the fingers crumbled. Pfoundes raised his broken stone fingers to his deeply-socketed eyes in which the dark gleam lurked, and moaned at his hand of stone thumbs, and flexed them. They crumbled further, and dark cracks ran up his arm and all over his body, over his stone suit, which started to drop off in sections. The cracks spread over his face, so that it seemed hideously veined, and blood poured in a torrent from them. As Pfoundes writhed, stone and blood dropped away so that there was nothing but a heap of rubble left behind in the hollow bright space of the star.

Then the rubble stirred and fell aside, and there was a smaller statue of Pfoundes among the broken stones, struggling to turn over the pages in his great book, moaning through sealed lips from the corner of which a little blood flowed, cracking himself, and the pieces falling down into the star. A second time the pieces of bloody stone fell aside, revealing a still smaller statue, but this one did not struggle with its page. It looked fixedly out of the screen, and then began to run towards them.

A cameraman in the aisle was struggling against his will with one of the heavy shoulder-held cameras. His face was scarlet and blood poured out of his nose down his front. His eyes were closed. He propped the camera-bracket on his shoulder and pointed the lens at the Oscilloscope screen that showed the running Pfoundes, who seemed to leap out of his machine into the TV camera. Immediately the monitors at the back of the room fill with life and colour. A newsreader is seated at his desk, commenting on a riot shown on back-projection. The only sound is that of rushing foetal heartbeats rustling and galloping. The newsreader turns towards an image behind him of a youth attacking a bearded policeman with a broken bottle. He turns back, and he has Pfoundes' grave and confident consulting-room face. Pfoundes works his lips, pleased that they will open, looks straight at the room, and with a level-eyed newsreader's look says 'The Dead live, and they live in . . .' but before he can finish, the channel switches to a chorus-line of women who are singing. They all turn in unison, kicking up net-stockinged legs, and when they turn back they all have Pfoundes' consulting-room face, and he is singing gravely to the sound of a squeeze-box and a drum beating in unison with the foetal heartbeats, 'The Dead live, and they live in . . .' and before they can finish the channel switches again.

This time a conjurer is shown and he is putting a lady wearing evening dress and diamonds into a tall box. He closes the lid and with many smiles and brilliant grimaces plunges a set of cavalry sabres into the sides and front of the box. Occasionally he meets resistance, but with a struggle he gets the sword through. We see that the further portions of the blades are bloodstained, and blood is trickling out of the foot of the box. Now the conjurer notices this, and with a change of expression he begins hurriedly to pull the steel out. It rings as he withdraws it. The foetal heartbeat is approaching again, drowning all other sounds. Pfoundes flings open the lid of the conjurer's cabinet and steps out, her gown rent and her wounds bleeding. 'The Dead live, and they live in . . .' he-she begins, and then Angela from the medium's chair gives a shriek of agony. It pulls the

151

image of Pfoundes in her blue-and-bloody gown out of the screen, though she clasps the cabinet to prevent herself going — but that is on castors, and slides — then she grasps the conjurer, who repudiates her, and she is whisked out of the picture and seems to travel across the air straight into Angela's mouth, which is wide open with her cry. Her face lengthens and her hair withdraws into the scalp and goes glossy, her body enlarges and splits her clothes, and Pfoundes is standing there looking down at his rags. He raises his face and looks about him triumphantly. He looks about at the open-mouthed journalists, and beckons to the bloody-nosed cameraman to bring his lens closer. All in the room have lost themselves in the emotion of these events, like a play or a contest between forces separated from them by the abyss of death or the glassy surface of the Oscilloscope and television screens, but now the fact itself has stepped into the room. John Ismay has fallen to his knees and is praying. Several of the journalists follow suit, leaning their faces against the high backs of the gilt chairs in front of them, just as if they were in church. Pfoundes — if it is him and not the Devil — smiles slowly, and begins to speak the words that will change the world. The Oscilloscope behind him shows a triptych of him on its three screens. 'The Dead live. The Dead live and they live in . . .'

Once again, before he can finish he is interrupted, but by his own machine this time. While maintaining its triptych of images, between which he stands as a fourth, the Oscilloscope's speakers are sending out *silence*. The risen Pfoundes' lips move, but there is no sound. Then, very faintly, hoofbeats come galloping towards them in the utter silence, and with the hoofbeats are little moans, little moans that have relief and pleasure in them, and pain and expectation. Pfoundes looks about him for the source of the sound, as if reminding himself that he is backed by his own power, the Oscilloscope. He sees the switch-gear on the armrest of the couch, and moves quickly across to it to turn his treacherous machine off. Ismay is there before him, and with a face of terror grapples with the ghost before it can reach the 'off' switch. Red man and corpse-white spirit wrestle over the couch. Meanwhile the speakers are sending out their swift and distant hoofbeat sound, and the moans are still there, but the latter are not in the speaker. They are in the room, and among the audience. A big floppy hat and a flowered frock is rocking back and forth in the third row: the pregnant lady journalist is in labour. Many hands rush to her aid; the spell of the conflict on the stage is forgotten, and willing hands lift the gently-moaning lady with the deeply-concentrated face through the chairs and on to the couch of the Pfoundes Oscilloscope. It is that or the floor: she must have her baby in the best conditions available. The struggle between ghost and medium is forgotten: Ismay and Angela in her tattered clothes stand aside: there is no sign of Pfoundes. The elderly spiritualist turns out to be a doctor as well, and he dispatches his wife to the kitchen for linen and hot water, and the theatre critic of the *Sunday Excellent* to the car for his bag, which arrives quickly. Carefully the elderly spiritualist runs his hands over the body of the woman in labour stretched out on the comfortable chair now extended to its fully-reclining position. He puts the earpieces of his stethoscope in, and moves its disc over her belly. As he does so, the sound of the galloping

153

foetal heartbeat drains from the room. The doctor lifts his head. 'It's all right,' he says, 'the heartbeat is very strong.'

Pfoundes' face appears once more on the Oscilloscope screens, looking anxiously out at the bustle of people, who are too busy to notice him. The screen goes dark once again, and a single star approaches, with the rushing, galloping sound. 'Turn that damned thing down,' shouts the doctor, and somebody does so. The image still shows, and the light rushes closer. Pfoundes is hanging upside down in the screen. His head is large and his body small, and his tiny hands are struggling with a little book. It slips from them, and floats a few inches from his face, turning over its own pages. He gives a visible sigh, and relaxes, his eyes close, and, his great triple-stranded umbilicus coiling, he is sucked into the birth-passage that takes his head and his whole body and squeezes it gently as he descends. The screen is empty now, but there is a squalling from the couch as the doctor delivers the baby and puts it into its radiant mother's arms, wrapped in a kitchen towel. The Oscilloscope has gone dead, not a flicker on its screen, and stands there like an ancient altar of burnished metal and empty frames. The mother rubs her nipple over the lips of the newborn child, and it sucks the first few precious drops. Angela presses through the crowd of smiling people, and the mother looks up at her. Silently she unfolds the towel and shows Angela that she has given birth to a perfectly ordinary baby girl.

* * *

'I think this is a dangerous and unnecessary experiment, and, I do believe, useless, because no post-hypnotic suggestion will take if it's so against the will of the subject. And I am deeply against it, Father. I think it is vainglorious to wish to use another person so. Father?' His head was deep in his pillow like a hood. It was as though he had turned to stone. His mouth was open and his tongue quite dry. His forehead to her touch was as cold as stone. She got up from the couch where she had slept his death through, and drew the curtains. It was a sunny day, and the postman was just coming up the drive with a morning's clutch of fresh white letters in his hand.

Note on Hypnotism

Those who doubt that hypnotism is capable of the kind of effects described in this novel should consult, for instance, *Hypnosis and Behaviour Modification: Imagery Conditioning*, by William S. Kroger and William D. Fezler (Philadelphia, J. B. Lippincott, 1976). But, of course, nobody has invented the Pfoundes Oscilloscope — yet.

Hypnotism in its milder form is accessible to everyone who cares to look up qualified hypnotists in the yellow pages. One should ask the therapist to give one a 'post-hypnotic suggestion for self-hypnosis'. One may then explore one's abilities in this area at one's leisure. The experience of trance, properly managed, is a very pleasant one, exactly like those sensitive and imaginative times when one floats naturally in the blissful state between sleeping and waking. Even a poor hypnotic subject may derive great benefit from the relaxation, and gain skill from faithful practice. The majority of people are good hypnotic subjects, and exploration may uncover useful and interesting skills, including clairvoyance, natural childbirth, and dream-control under post-hypnotic suggestion.